CW00705685

Copyright © Win Adams
First published in Great Britain 2010
Printed and Published by PDQ Print Services
www.pdqprint.co.uk

A CIP catalogue record for this title is available from
the British Library

ISBN 978-0-9542667-3-8

WriteDirect
writedirect@aol.com

To Jean once more
For her continuing love, sympathy and patience

My grateful appreciation and thanks
to John Low, John McCraw and Ken Moore
who patiently read and corrected my manuscript
and offered their welcome advice.

For Nicky, Lauren and Jean
Who read the initial chapters.

OPEN VERDICT

WIN ADAMS

For what is a verdict
Without the bitter sweet bite of revenge?
And the lasting sorrow, the wasted life.

MONDAY

CHAPTER ONE

I don't know what it was that took me away from dad for a couple of days, but I found myself in Edinburgh, standing near to a young American woman.

It was not to be till much later that I learned the story of that young American widow, standing at the ramparts high on the plug of that old extinct volcano that cradled Edinburgh Castle, the wind in her blond hair, as she and I stared out at the view below.

The gunner was scanning the Time-Ball above the Nelson Monument way across on Calton Hill, with the 105mm field gun primed and ready for its ritual one o'clock firing.

The woman looked first to the west, towards the airport. Then I saw her gaze ahead out over Waverley Bridge, the Scott Monument and Princes Street.

But finally she stared north towards the waters of the Firth of Forth, beyond them the lands of Fife and the road to

St Andrews in this 150th year of the Open Championship. It was just then that the cannon went off.

The woman dropped something on to the parapet and lunged forward. She must have been holding the thing for some time.

I thought she was going to throw herself over. I grabbed her and trapped the thing under my coat sleeve.

In the moment before we both recovered and laughed at our reactions and my misunderstanding, I glanced at what she'd dropped. It was a gold ring.

Before I handed it back to her I noticed engraved on the inside the words: *R Brand to Lisa, Boston*. Then the imprint of a small aircraft.

She looked straight into my eyes.

"Thank you so much. My husband Robert gave it to me before we married. He ran his own company. *Brand Avionics*. But he and my son were both killed in an air crash. And now I haven't a friend in the world."

Her talk of death, the admission that she felt so alone, came so suddenly, so unexpectedly, and shook me.

The woman looked away again as the tears welled up in her eyes.

I couldn't help myself. I touched her arm, gave her my mobile number, the very least I could do, I thought and said, "Call my cellphone if you want. Any time, right?" I felt totally inadequate, a real jerk. But what else could I do?

Anyway, a few moments later she appeared to have controlled herself, though she wouldn't look me in the eye now. A small scene, two casual strangers and only lasting a few brief moments in a foreign land.

In the end I might just have seen her lips move as she whispered to herself, though the words were barely audible, were not directed at anyone I could see, least of all me and made little sense at the time.

"You've been judged and you'll pay. I'll make sure you pay. In full!"

I didn't understand what she meant.

I watched as she turned and walked away, along the castle courtyard, to vanish down into the narrows of the Royal Mile. And I thought that was the end of our meeting.

At the same time and unknown to me that day, in St Andrews, that historic town on Scotland's East Coast, another judgment was being issued.

This time by another grieving witness, my dad Jack Granger, standing at the window of his room in the Old Course Hotel and looking down towards the 18th hole.

That day, as he confessed to me later, dad was thinking that the power that he had to overcome now lay partly in the Open Championship itself but also in this 18th Hole of the renowned Old Course. A hole steeped in history, imbued and guarded with a force and mystery all its own.

At one end of the 18th stands one edifice, the redstone bulk and splendour of Hamilton Hall, one-time *Grand Hotel*, one time university student residence vibrant with the hopes and aspirations of the carefree young. Eerily quiet and empty at the moment, this institution sits and waits, safe in the knowledge it is soon to be refurbished, resurrected, reincarnated, clad with flesh and blood and life once more.

At the other end of the 18th lies the Old Course Hotel. Vibrant, rich, vigorous, gloriously surveying the land, sea and sky around, filled to the rafters.

Packed to capacity with the spectators of this world. With the idly curious, attracted by the beauty and drama to come. With the great and the good. And of course, with the cream of the golfing profession.

And there stood that man, my dad, the golfer Jack Granger, one of the elite, the chosen of his profession.

For the most part they are mortals, these golfers, men of hope, some of greed, of vitality, aspirants to glory, drinking in the beauty, the temptations and the drama that will envelop them.

But mere mortals, I thought, when all was said and done. Almost all would fall victim to the course in the end. All but one single, lucky winner.

And like the widow I had seen at the Edinburgh castle walls it was Jack Granger at his hotel window who now made a vow, I learned, vowed with all his strength and mind to be that single winner.

And more important, to win back his wife. And redeem himself.

Both contestants, the unknown woman I had seen briefly in Edinburgh and this man, my father in St Andrews, were to be strangely linked as they each prepared for their role in the momentous events of the days to come, the week of the 150th anniversary of the British Open Golf Championship.

That day I could see no connection, could not begin to understand the past that had ensnared them both, or the future that would carry them forward in the week to come.

But here is the story that would unfold.

TUESDAY

CHAPTER TWO

It began first with a body. A body face down in the water of the Swilcan Burn. Nearer the Old Course Hotel than Hamilton Hall, and under that little stone Swilcan bridge so renowned in the life and history of the Old Course.

But I am moving too fast, too far ahead. I must introduce myself.

I am Amy, Amy Granger, 18 year-old daughter of John Millar Granger. We are here, the two of us dad and I, but not my mother, Laura Anne Granger. We are here for the golf.

The golf! That is an understatement! For our family, reduced to just the two of us as it is now, golf and above all the Open is life and all it means for John Granger, called Jack. His mightiest challenge, especially in this its 150th celebration year in which his wife has left him, left us and so much of his life in particular seems destroyed. We seem, how can I describe it, possessed, taken over, victims almost. Yet I know we'll fight. I know dad has wound himself up for a fight, a most almighty fight. To the death you might say. So be it.

Possessed, we seem possessed by this life, by the past and now also by the present.

The Open, this particular Open, takes over everything. The organisers take over everything. The starter himself is theirs, even if the St Andrews links clubhouse, bar and restaurant remain the possession of the members, players and associated staff.

These organisers, these smaller guardians of the Open oblige me, Amy Granger, daughter of the renowned Jack Granger, oblige me to have a badge to get around.

And the cost of things! A cappuccino here cost me 2.90 today.

This Tuesday after my day in Edinburgh I'm sitting alone at the window of the smaller New Course Links Clubhouse, because from here I can survey most of the scene.

I must say the view from here, as I look back up over towards the historic West Sands on my left, over the hilly putting green in front of me, then further away towards the 1st tee and the Clubhouse of the Royal and Ancient, the R&A with its wall plaque bust of old Tom Morris, the view is stunning, enthralling. Yet it possesses me. Still years later it comes unbidden to my mind.

I can see a window cleaner there by the R&A wall. This cleaner sees it all. All that is around him. In some ways he seems an important man.

Sees into the R&A clubhouse rooms, where an old man

at a table is studiously reading the *Times*, binoculars on the table on which he has spread his newspaper. In the morning light of those tall narrow windows in those high ceilinged clubrooms, one fan is turning slowly, lazily above.

The window cleaner sees it all. And of course further back still the sight of Hamilton Hall, with its view down over the fairways, Links Road and the Old Course Hotel, has made his day. And mine.

Way across to my right, I can see workmen at one of the windows of our hotel, the Old Course. Their truck sits downstairs not far from the Swilcan burn and its bridge. Reception told me when I came out of the hotel this morning they are part of a media contract to upgrade the television reception for the hotel.

From here where I sit I can also trace the view clear up from our Old Course View deluxe suite and our balcony, to the Swilcan bridge and beyond. Over the past few days while dad and his caddy George Orr have toiled and planned, my partner Greg, freelance reporter, and I have tasted the delights of the Old Course Hotel restaurant, not to mention the Jigger Inn, and the malts of the Road Hole Bar.

Then there's Greg. Not with me at this moment, though he usually is. He likes to wander.

I'm not sure if I love Greg or not.

So much has happened and is happening now, that I don't know if it's just the place, this magical old place and the times we live in. So much is happening, changing. But I think I love him. And I know I miss my mom.

But if the golf and all of the hotel's delights find me still jaded, heaven forbid, the M90 lies close by, leading north to Angus, Perth and the Highlands, or south to Edinburgh where I went yesterday. Edinburgh, its castle, its High Street and its airport.

And I can travel around as I wish. Dad has told me to enjoy. Not to get down and morose, even if mom's no longer with us. So I won't.

Some mornings like this Greg and I have strolled for a change across the fairway from the Old Course Hotel to this Links Clubhouse where we have coffee and take in the view. Then we walk and try to gauge the scene. But this morning Greg has wandered off and left me to my own thoughts.

All this should delight me. Yet it still manages me, controls me. I just don't feel free today.

Some may condemn me for not enjoying completely the luxuries and delights around me, around the Old Course. Yet here there is a different atmosphere. Yes, believe me. Here there can be demons for some, despite the scenes of beauty and opulence and seeming charm, with this mixture of antiquity and history and romance.

Here there is tension.

Maybe it's just me but I can see it in my father. I can see it in others too. Excruciating, nerve wracking tension. Tension with a capital T. Yet people here, some of them, would not be without it.

And this is not just a story about golf or golfers. It is much more, believe me.

But back to the body.

Down from the path that is called Granny Clark's Wynd and the Swilcan Burn with its old stone bridge, the body in the burn later that day was just the first instance of the great tension and terrors that suddenly were to rear up and shatter the fragile self-confidence of our family.

CHAPTER THREE

It was the same day, Tuesday of that week in July, but just before eleven o'clock that night, I remember. One day before the final practice round and two days before the first day's play in the Old Course Open Golf Championship. But again, first things first.

My dad, as I said, is the golfer Jack Granger. For the purposes of this story I'll call him Granger, like most people do.

When Granger used his pass key and burst into our Old Course Hotel suite that night and snapped the light on, I was in bed with my partner Greg. When I'm with dad I never know whether to share a room, a bed, with Greg. But this time I did. I love my dad. And respect him. Wouldn't embarrass him for the world. And Lord knows he has enough worries at the moment.

I hurriedly tried to rearrange my nightie and look normal, though I was a little embarrassed. But then, that's me, and maybe I am like any young person in love. Like you were, once.

I struggled to pat my hair back into some shape. My six-foot partner Greg swung his legs out of bed and reached for a dressing gown.

Granger seemed hardly to notice us and slumped down onto the edge of the bed, clutching his laptop. I pulled myself up and Greg came round to sit beside me.

I looked at Greg and read his eyes. We were, after all, engaged and yet strangely embarrassed now. Greg had wanted the engagement, to do things the old-fashioned way and since he was 23 and I was 18 I had supposed he was right. But then a seemingly old-fashioned Englishman like Greg could hardly keep his hands off an American girl from Boston like me.

So we had got engaged. He said he loved me. I felt in love with him.

Give Greg his due, he gathered his wits quickly now.

"You look awful Granger. What on earth's the matter?"

Dad was drawn and pale with shock. "It's scared the hell out of me, I can hardly believe it!"

The events he told us of were surely horrendous, demonic.

CHAPTER FOUR

That night Granger had been standing by the window as he often does on tour, half looking outside, half watching the large tv. screen in his third floor adjoining suite in the Old Course Hotel.

As usual he had recorded on his laptop the evening tv coverage of the practice golf that day and his Vaio laptop dvd was still continuing to record. It was sometime before eleven and darkness had fallen.

Suddenly the program was interrupted and a body appeared on the tv screen, a woman lying face down on one arm in the Swilcan Burn, under the little arched bridge some 300 yards from dad's hotel room window.

Once he realised where the actual tv scene was, Granger had moved closer to the window to see both the tv screen and the actual incident outside.

Rain was falling, drifting in from the North Sea on an east wind. Police tape cordonned off the scene below. Oddly enough the blue light of the ambulance was not flashing but there were still garish shadows at times across the quiet flow of the burn, the bridge, two police cars in the background, and further back the lone television van.

There were no other spectators or people around but then I suppose it was late.

Granger said he had watched closely as the body was quickly and efficiently removed from the burn, and laid briefly on an ambulance stretcher. Briefly that is, before a white sheet was drawn over the body, and the face.

But not quite quickly enough, for the tv cameraman had leaned forward, capturing for Granger's tv screen the body and the still, white face.

And it was the face that suddenly became etched in Granger's mind. The face of a woman he thought he recognised.

A woman he used to know.

My mother.

His wife, Laura.

The shock hit Granger and he had sat down abruptly on his hotel bed.

Still the screen showed the scene below. The tv cameraman had been moved back. Two men with a stretcher carried the body away. The open ambulance rear doors swung shut and the vehicle moved off.

It was still raining, dad noticed, despite the mindless daze he found himself in. The blue, red and white lights of the vehicles around were haloed and glistening. Yet none were flashing. And the *ASIS* tv van sat there, its large tilted antenna presumably still beaming out the shots from the cameraman as he followed the scene.

As if in a dream Granger had stood up and moved in panic to the window. The actual scene below to his right was surreal, despite the reality around. The night air, the thin film of rain, the narrow Links Road parked with vehicles up all its length along the fairway towards the 18th green and up to Hamilton Hall.

Granger had stood shocked and mesmerised.

When was the last time he had seen his wife, Laura?

Three months ago almost. Yes, in early May. When he was carefree. And famous.

He still was famous. But not as he had been earlier, three months back, or years ago when he was 34. 34 years old and Open champion. For the second time, back to back. A hero, a cult figure, with Laura, his beautiful wife, and his daughter. Their daughter. Me, Amy. On top of the world.

Watching Granger's face I knew his mind had gone back to the past, a past not so long ago. One night past in May this year in Boston, Massachusetts, Laura had disappeared. Just like that. And no one knew where, or how, or why. Least of all my dad Jack Granger.

How I had suffered then! Dad's golf had suffered. My father Jack Granger had suffered. Fits of anger, moodiness, odd behaviour. Suffered more than anyone had known.

And just a moment ago she had reappeared. Laura. His wife, my mother. Live, if that was the right word for a woman in a stream, and on the tv screen in this hotel. And also outside this very hotel in fact, not 300 yards from us. Had reappeared and now had vanished again. Carried off in an ambulance. Motionless.

In a daze still, Granger told us how he had recorded most of it on his dvd laptop recorder, recorded it, stopped it, replayed it and was now struggling to force his mind to function.

His wife, Laura. Or was it?

He laid down his laptop, started the dvd again at the beginning, then played it and we all watched.

The initial brief shot caught by the enterprising cameraman was in fact of the body still in the water. One arm spread out, her head lying on the other arm, long, black hair fanned out against the sandy, reed bottom, undulating slowly in the quiet water of the Swilcan burn. The head lay turned to one side. In peace.

And then the shot was gone.

Granger had played it back from the start, three, four times. It was Laura, wasn't it? But the hair, black? But hair can be dyed. No, surely it was his wife?

Hurriedly he had shut off the Sony, and rushed for our room along the corridor, his mind a blank. And for a fleeting second I had selfishly thought: such a thing, and the night before the last practice tee-off in the Open tomorrow morning.

Granger was hardly making sense now.

He certainly had not watched events, as absolutely everything outside had been quickly cleared away from the Swilcan scene and inside the tv channel returned to normal.

Nor had he or anyone else seen as twenty minutes later a

man led the three security guards for the area out of the Jigger Inn, where he had jovially entertained them and kept them distracted for the past fifty minutes.

CHAPTER FIVE

As Granger, Greg and I ran from our room and rushed into the hotel lobby, we almost cannoned into two policemen, glistening yellow pull-ons over their uniforms.

One held up a hand.

"Can I help, Mr Granger?"

Stuttering and almost incoherent, dad spoke up, explaining what he had seen, aware of just how disjointed his statement was.

"No problem, sir. There's a taxi outside. I'll instruct the driver where to take you. Just leave it to us. This way please."

The policeman seemed at first to allow only Granger into the taxi, but after a glance from his colleague he allowed me and Greg to accompany dad. Somehow that seemed strange to me, that glance, and later significant. But not until later. And later, when Greg thought about it, the taxi too seemed odd.

The taxi drew up at the hospital, wherever that was. There was a delay while someone made sure dad was who he claimed to be. Jack Granger, the famous American golfer, holder of two Open titles, here for the Open. And that he thought the woman from the burn was his lost wife.

They led us inside. They took us down. Down to a quiet white room. To a gurney, where a form lay, covered from head to toe by a still, white sheet.

Granger was vaguely aware of someone saying to him," Of course you can't touch her, sir."

A pause. Then," Can I just ask you to identify her, sir, if you can?"

Granger had nodded, dumbstruck and senseless.

The sheet was pulled back. The face appeared. And the long black hair. No blonde roots, we saw.

Laura. I saw tears on dad's cheeks, and he wiped at them with the back of a hand.

He groaned.

But then he noticed. It was not there.

Laura had always had faith in him, that he would be a champion, and after his first Open victory, those six years ago, she had triumphantly reminded him of her birthmark that looked like a jug. Despite himself he had smiled at her insistence. A small birthmark. At the base of her neck, just above her spine.

Yet it did bear some resemblance to the Claret Jug, the mark of an Open Championship winner.

And now there was no sign of it on the body. It was not

there.

As I watched, Granger steeled himself, bent forward, and looked more carefully. No, not there. The birth mark was definitely not there.

He stepped back, seemingly recovering, then shocked and feeling so guilty to be relieved at the death of another. He shook his head.

"It's not Laura," he mumbled. "Not Laura. Not my wife."

"Are you sure, sir?" It was the young doctor who had spoken, taking him gently by the arm. "Quite sure?" and looking up anxiously into Jack Granger's eyes, his tear-streaked face.

I watched as dad nodded.

"It's not her. I'm sure of it. Sorry. So sorry." And he turned away.

I vaguely heard voices behind us as we left the mortuary. "Well, he should know after all, shouldn't he? He's her husband."

And another voice.

"The eve of an Open does strange things to you, though. You know. And so late at night. He's good, brilliant in fact, but how can even he play a practice round tomorrow and then a championship after all this?"

And a third speaker, just as we drifted out of range of the voices.

" Tees off tomorrow morning. 8.01 am. Last practice round, but even so. Better him than me."

The voices were still ringing in our ears as we stumbled away, out from the low mortuary block. Out and away.

Up into the cool air and the slanting drizzle.

The sky quite dark now, fresh, wet. Yet clean, and life giving.

It was not her.

Someone got the three of us a cab. Later we could hardly remember returning to the Old Course Hotel. We went with dad upstairs and into his room.

Granger, the famous Jack Granger decided to go right to bed, assuring us he'd be ok though I thought he'd have trouble getting to sleep. How little I knew my dad.

I crossed the room to draw the Venetian blinds and I noticed from his window the scene outside the hotel, down by the Swilcan burn bridge.

It was as if nothing at all had happened. The crime scene tape had gone. The police had gone, no ambulance of course, and strangely perhaps no tv van either.

All gone. As if it had never been.

CHAPTER SIX

Downstairs in the lounge of the Old Course Hotel Greg and I sat down with dad's manager, Mark Meekin. We slumped into the deep leather chairs at the reception area's far corner table.

The two policemen I had seen earlier in the lobby seemed to have gone, but then, I realised, all that must have been quite some time ago now.

I looked up at Meekin.

"How do you think he is, Mark?"

Meekin rubbed his eyes and looked slowly, carefully at my face before he replied.

"Jack's fine, I think. Must have been a great shock, of course. But he also seemed relieved. Frankly he has enough on his plate to deal with without all that. But you got him to bed and I had a quick look in at him later. He seems to have fallen asleep. There were still a couple of men, police technicians or somebody like that, about to leave his room. Good of them to check it out like that. But like I said, they went out, and everything seems ok now. I hope.

"Went into my suite along the corridor to check on things. No problem there. Night manager is checking your room too. Seems fine. I'm glad you went with Granger to the mortuary. God, I could do with a drink. Can we get one here?"

Greg nodded, held up a hand, and a waiter came and took our order. A Bushmills for Meekin, a good strong California Pinot Noir for Greg and me.

For a minute we sipped in silence.

"He said the woman looked like his wife. That's what set him off," Greg said at last.

"Figures," I replied. "Laura's departure in Boston hit him hard. She just upped and went in May, no reason, no goodbye. Never did understand it. How about you, Mark?"

Meekin shook his head.

"Me neither. Granger never spoke really to me about it as he did to you, though it affected him badly up until they re-confirmed his automatic entry for the Open here and that seemed to perk him up. The British Open and the 150th anniversary championship in particular mean a lot.

Everything must have got to Laura in the end though, I suppose, despite the many times she and you spent together. Maybe she's gone off to the high plains country. Great climber she is, rock climbing in Montana and so many other places round the US. The two of you loved the climbing, didn't you Amy?

"But all that other stuff, those years of golf, that travelling, one country after another, one golf championship after another must have got to Laura. Yet another town, another hotel, airports, fancy women all around, cameramen, paparazzi, no private life of your own, and she trying to bring you up at the same time. No life at all for a woman. Or for a man."

Mark sighed, gulped at his drink.

"Hey, tell me about it!" he continued. "It's bad enough for me, his manager, though I'm not complaining. Not yet anyways."

"But it must have built up, then hit her all of a sudden. And so Laura left him. Left you."

Meekin shook his head.

"Granger seemed to have got over it, accepted it, up till tonight. Coming back onto some of the best golf he's ever played, I tell you, Amy."

A brief smile lit up Meekin's suntanned face.

"And he's got it in him to do well here in the Open, like he did before, like the two Opens years ago. I'd bet on it!"

We sat in silence for a few more minutes till our drinks were finished. Finally we all went up to bed, thinking of the last practice day to come and then the championship ahead, Thursday through Sunday.

WEDNESDAY

CHAPTER SEVEN

In October of the previous year, as I discovered later, a woman, that woman on the Edinburgh Castle ramparts, had flown from Vancouver to Manchester, then continued on up to Edinburgh in Scotland.

On arrival at Edinburgh airport on a cold dismal morning she placed her backpack in left luggage and wandered around the airport for the next few hours.

Entering the multi storey carpark she took the stairs to the top floor. Crossing the roof to the far east side, she had a magnificent view of the former Turnhouse airfield and the new buildings constructed there.

To her right she clearly made out three luxury private jets near the Air Enhance terminal buildings. And it was these that held her attention. One of these, she saw to her satisfaction, was a Learjet.

She took the elevator back to the ground floor and walked over to the Hilton. There she treated herself to lunch then continued her survey, leaving the Hilton by the rear exit and walking up the curve of the road past the open-air car Park and around towards the company she had researched online, Air Enhance.

She spent some time there checking out the buildings and using her digital Canon to record the various types of aircraft for hire dispersed round the hard stands.

It was nearly 3 p.m. when she finally retrieved her backpack and took the double-decker shuttlebus to the terminus at Waverley bridge.

From there she followed the instructions in the Edinburgh guide on her iPhone and took a taxi up and round into the Royal Mile where she asked to be dropped by the side door to St Giles Cathedral. Crossing the cobbles near Roxburgh's Close she entered the front door of the old stone building there and collected her key for the temporary flat she had secured online. She had arranged for ten months lodgings in an apartment three floors up.

The following morning she phoned the private air company she had checked out the day before at the rear of the Edinburgh Airport Hilton, as the receptionist I spoke to later confirmed. She had e-mailed to the company, Air Enhance, the copy she had prepared of her cv and arranged an interview for herself at 10.30 a.m. two days later.

On her digital camera she must have rehearsed and re-rehearsed a mock interview till she believed she had it perfect.

At 10.25 that day, so I was told, she presented herself at the offices of Air Enhance and after a flawless interview and a whole afternoon spent verifying her credentials and practical skills she obtained a year's contract as flight engineer and copilot.

She took up one of their private rental jets the following day it seems, and again the day after on a longer flight. The company declared itself satisfied, well pleased in fact to get such a skilled co-pilot and qualified flight engineer at such short notice, as the receptionist also told me.

Air Enhance would also provide minibus transport daily from Edinburgh centre to their location at Edinburgh Airport and their separate location at the adjacent private air facility, Turnhouse, as I was to learn at the end.

The long months of planning and preparation were now over and the next part of her plan had been set in motion. Every morning from October to July she must have risen with her alarm, leaving her flat above Roxburgh's Close in Edinburgh's High Street at 7.05 and taking her daily *Boston Globe* from the news rack at International Newsagents nearby. Each day she would have turned left and walked down the pavement alongside the inverted sand bucket shapes of the traffic guards.

She would have passed the historic line of Edinburgh's Closes, from Warriston's and Mary King's by the pillars of the City Chambers, down the length of the Royal Mile towards the old Tron Kirk and the Fleshmarket Close.

There she crossed the cobbles to Starbucks, then retraced her steps, back across the road, cupping her hands round the coffee and donut, to wait by the Woollen Mill store at the top of Cockburn Street.

At 7.15 by each of the Old Tron's clock faces the Air Enhance minibus would round the corner at the top of South Bridge, turn first left into the High Street, then right and pull up by the Woollen Mill.

The sliding door would open and she got in, always choosing the furthermost rear seat. The door slid to and the minibus would proceed on its way down the slope of Cockburn, past the vans parked on the kerb by the *Malt Shovel* and a gaudy row of dresses hung high outside on the window of *PIE IN THE SKY* to reach the final curve of the road, with Warriston's stairs and railing on one side and a brief glimpse of the Scott Monument and Waverley Bridge up on the right, before the minibus joined Market Street.

And so, in less than two weeks after arriving at Edinburgh and still under her maiden name she had obtained at the lowest rate of salary a temporary job as co-pilot and flight engineer with FlightEnhance Air Services, UK, at Turnhouse, Edinburgh Airport.

Her mini bus would finally drive down the long straight length of Turnhouse Road, past parked transport trucks then fields of corn with a red-berried rowan trees and sycamores to finally turn in at the security gate of the air cargo and private aircraft's section of Turnhouse at Edinburgh Airport.

"M'am," the security guard told me when I asked about her at the end, "she always got out of the minibus last of all, and she always spoke. We'd have a quick chat like

'The Learjet 95 is due for a rollout and short test flight today. So you have a bit of a walk to dispersal!' I would smile and tick off the check sheet on my clip board. 'She's on the hard stand across there,' I would say, pointing to the southwest of the airfield. She always spent a lot of time and paid great attention to that Learjet. Charlie'll give you a lift out to the Lear in his Ford transit. Oh, and look out your co-pilot logbook. Air Traffic Control want to confirm things with you." Yeah, we always had a chat and she was so nice. Little sad, though. Never much of a smile out of her. Never mind."

And so, as I learned, she finished the final mile to the Air Enhance Learjet 95, to the hard standing where her employer now of two months, Air Enhance Services, were beginning their final checks on the aircraft. Apparently every morning it was the same, Monday to Saturday, returning at 6.30 every evening, getting off at the junction of Market and Cockburn, to climb the many steps of Warriston's to Roxburgh's narrow stone-blocked exit opposite St Giles at the top.

And working every night in the flat on the electronic remote she was building. Every evening that was. And most weekends too.

But now it was July. The day she had planned for so carefully was coming. The day that would change everything.

CHAPTER EIGHT

It was early Wednesday morning, after that awful Tuesday night and the body in the burn.

The very worst of e-mails had arrived on dad's cellphone. It came with an attachment, a video clip. We watched it to the end until it stopped and that final shot remained frozen onscreen, seemingly immobilising us.

The three of us, Granger, Greg and I watched the video several times over. We made a few tentative deductions from what we had seen.

The film itself seemed to have been taken deliberately on a very average camcorder or on the cellphone camera itself, with almost no sound and poor resolution. It gave few details about the room and location.

The deliberate use of a blindfold on the only person in view was intended no doubt to unnerve Granger and force him to comply.

It sure unnerved me.

The seemingly rehearsed speech by Laura, for it was plainly Laura, dad's Laura and my mom, showed even more the constraint that had been applied to her.

The fact that she was bound hand and foot to a plain, hard, uncomfortable chair beside a bed in a very sparse, unfurnished room reinforced the idea of compulsion and the fear and pain her imprisonment must be causing her. That morning's *Times* newspaper near her confirmed the date.

The fact that a short document and the video clip were attached to a mobile phone e-mail message dated that morning showed some familiarity and skill by the sender. Yet the anonymity of the sender was a clever concealment and his or her location could be yards away or thousands of miles off, I thought.

And yet it proved untraceable. And the words in the document warning us not to try a trace or to seek help of any kind, especially from the police, were chilling and convincing enough.

It could be a house, a room in a hotel, an apartment, here in this town of St. Andrews, or in Edinburgh, or for that matter far away in Boston, Granger's home town.

Everything seemed to give dad and the two of us no hope, no information, no choice other than to comply.

And yet as I pointed out, the sender had inadvertently used two different terms. 'Cellphone', and then later, 'mobile'. Did that mean the person was used to American terminology and yet was basically British? A small ray of hope, perhaps.

And what did the words Laura had spoken, "play well in the Open. But not too well to win" imply?

Was that a plea, or a warning to ensure that Granger would show no one else the stress he was playing under? In the months before then we had assumed Laura had just walked out on Granger, on us. Now we knew different. At least that was a relief.

But it was clear now she'd been abducted, coerced and was being held against her will, to force Granger to do as her captors wished in the Open. Why? Was Granger really that good? Was he actually still favourite and likely to win?

And what did not winning have to do with anything? Unless to prove that Granger's wife and her life meant more to him than just an Open title, a third Open title?

The 150th Open title though, I remember thinking to myself.

Yet, for all that we sat and talked and talked it over, round and about, we could make little else of it. All we could do, all Granger in fact could do, was obey. And keep quiet about it. For the sake of his wife's life. My mom's life.

I remember Greg looking at me. Dad and I were not our own persons now. Others were setting about controlling us.

CHAPTER NINE

After the video we had breakfast early quietly and carefully in dad's suite.

We said little, though I kept snatching glances at dad's face. He would be on tee at 8 am, 08.01 to be exact.

He seemed calm enough, ate steadily and thoughtfully, making little contribution to the desultory conversation Greg and I thought up to try and pass the time, to cover up the events of the previous night and the effect of the video e-mail. Looking back on it, he was a strong man, a man who managed to keep his feelings hidden.

Until Granger's cellphone, his mobile as Greg calls it, vibrated. Vibrated again, I should say.

Strange time to call Granger I thought, but it was a text message apparently, and I suppose dad gets plenty of those, well wishers mostly, encouraging him before he takes to the first tee.

But this was no ordinary text message.

Granger's face drained of blood and he seemed to grip the cellphone in horror, staring at the screen. He said not a word so I grabbed the thing from him and read the simple text message onscreen.

"That could have been her, you know. Could have been your wife, the woman in the burn last night, and then in the mortuary. I have your wife, as you have seen. She is safe and more or less well. For the moment. Do as I say and she will be returned, safe and alive. But do as I say. Play normal today, if you can. Play well tomorrow. Let them see no lack of confidence. Tell no one of what has happened. No one. Know what I'm saying? I shall be watching. Your job is to play well, qualify for the last two days of the championship, be here for the final Saturday and Sunday. And then we shall see."

No name, no sender, and no doubt sent on a throwaway pay-as-you-go cell phone.

Strangely we hardly discussed the text. Hardly said a word at all, the three of us, until dad's manager, Mark Meekin arrived and he and Granger went off to get caddie George Orr and make ready for Granger's warm-up and last practice.

CHAPTER TEN

As Granger and George Orr prepared to tackle the Old
Course for the last of the practice sessions, it never
occurred to either of them, or to me for that matter,
that their progress from the first tee was being watched
with great interest by a man who would not only invite
them out for the evening later that same day, but had
also actually walked the whole of that Old Course one
Sunday four weeks previously and would walk it again
today, following all Granger's play with interest.

As I made my exit from the clubhouse another voice
rang out, almost seeming to take over.
I felt now as if my life was ruled and directed by others.
Here stood an ebullient forceful looking man beside me.
"Well what a coincidence! I'm Diack. Alex Diack.
Amy Granger isn't it? I was just about to follow your
dad round myself. Here, let me walk with you and give
you my arm where you need it. And if you really need

it, we'll get a buggy."

I agreed to walk with him, especially as my partner Greg, my fiancé I suppose, had just left to go and check up quietly and discretely on the morgue and hospital in St Andrews and also the main hospital of Ninewells in the nearby city of Dundee, if he thought it necessary.

Greg had left just as I had, but out the main door of the hotel. He later told me he'd noticed a blond haired woman deliver a beautiful dark blue Cadillac Escalade with Massachusetts number plates to the hotel car park out front. Quite a beauty.

The car or the woman? I remember asking.

Both, was the answer. Typical.

Anyway I came back now to the present and it was this man Diack speaking again, looking up across the fairway to the 1st hole.

"We can walk up the path here and make it in time to join your dad at the second tee, I think. I see you've got a course permit like mine, so we can hurry across now, if its not to much of a strain for you."

It wasn't really, so off we set.

Diack was an amiable man, garrulous, I remember, and full of conversation. He seemed to start into his life story right away, without any prompting from me. Or maybe it was just to take my mind off myself. Even today I'm still not sure.

I remember looking ahead and seeing the big coloured figure of George Orr, dad's caddy, as they strode from the first green and made towards the second tee.

Orr seemed to be paying little attention to the other two

competitors in the three ball, I thought, as Diack and I approached. They would have to struggle with their thoughts as he and Granger were doing with their own. This was not a game of golf. It was a championship. An Open, at St. Andrews. A century and a half year old celebration.

Across in the group of spectators to his right Orr had noticed me and Diack. I could read Orr's thoughts. Orr's an old fashioned guy, his thoughts plain to read on his open face.

An older man, stocky, in his forties maybe, I'll bet Orr was thinking. He's always looking out for me, looking after me, like some chaperone or something. Not my partner Greg Walsh then, George would be thinking to himself. Did you call them partners these days? Partner sounded so unfriendly, Orr would be thinking to himself. So … well Orr didn't know what did he think about that. But then he was growing older. The word Orr preferred was boyfriend. Yes, boyfriend. Fiancé would be even better.

Better stop thinking like that, like a father. He was a caddy and Jack Granger's chauffeur. And yet mostly he felt like one of the family and was certainly treated like that by the Grangers, and especially by that girl he was looking across at. Me. Amy.

I watched Orr glance again at Granger, who seemed just slightly preoccupied. Orr knew a lot about my dad.

Granger had been brought up in Scotland. Only briefly though, for Granger's father Alan, my granddad, was an American who had served at the U. S. listening post in

Edzell in Angus not far from St Andrews.

Alan had married a local Scottish lass, Rebecca. Rebecca Thomson, which accounts I suppose for some of my English ways, if the Scots will forgive the word 'English'.

A son, Jack, had been born, then the Grangers had gone back to the father Allan's house in the town of Boston, Massachusetts.

The family had lived comfortably there in an old house on Beacon Hill, till one day Alan Granger had been accidentally killed in a road accident.

From then on the widow Rebecca Granger had brought up their only son, my dad Jack Granger.

Orr himself had been born in Texas, Austin, dad had told me, learning to play golf from his earliest years, and being good enough to get a job eventually as caddy to the ever increasing visitors of US and foreign golfers who came to test themselves against the elite course he worked at.

Some years passed and Jack Granger happened to see and then choose George Orr to caddy for him in the local state tournaments and eventually in his US Masters. Then after that his first British Open. Granger had gone on to win that Open competition, then the following one. No small feat. And he and big George Orr had became famous.

And now there they were again, as Diack and I hurried to catch up on them. And Jack Granger, two times winner of the Open already, was now favourite to win that title again in this special year, five years after his last back-to-back victory in it.

CHAPTER ELEVEN

As we started off along the second fairway, on the 395 yards of the hole they call *The Dyke*, I was surprised to find how strong and virile this man walking beside me was.

Alex Diack wore a light anorak and held a large multicoloured umbrella against the slight rain that had sprung out of the east. His fitness and muscular frame stood out for all around to see.

And boy did he have a real air of self-confidence, of wealth and experience I suppose. Life was pleasant for him and he seemed to be enjoying himself, as if he held some private secret, some joke that only he was aware of. It also looked like he was prepared to take on the world, to face up to anything that might come his way.

I should have been watching dad more closely, but he seemed to be playing well enough, unaffected apparently by the events of last night or the cellphone video and text.

Diack commented on what a fine golfer dad was. I was flattered, I suppose.

Diack spoke of this and that, of how keen an amateur golfer he was himself, when he got the time from his business in America, *Diack Technologies*.

Alexander John Diack was an entrepreneur. A self-made man.

Born in Scotland in 1970, as he told me, he had shown no particular aptitude at school and life at the age of 15, he told me.

His mother had died when he was 12 and his father, a hard-working and determined soul, had lost heart and moved out of town to live with his brother in the country. Alex Diack was made of sterner stuff. He had stayed behind in the city, went down to the local library where each day he read from cover to cover the local newspaper, writing down in a cheap notebook details of any job offers that came up.

The offer he had selected eventually was one from a company called *Melville Erskine*, a Scottish founded company, he assumed, and one that seemed to him to be engaged in roads, building and engineering.

For a whole fortnight the young Diack had haunted the library and read every book he could find, not just on *Melville Erskine*, but on engineering and road building in general.

To me he seemed a determined, organised man, even from his youngest days. Every evening after a frugal meal Alex Diack had planned his campaign.

The campaign was for his interview with *Melville Erskine*. He was determined to get an interview and even more determined to do well in that interview.

Came the Wednesday morning where he donned his best clothes, used all the money had saved to buy a ticket and boarded a bus for Edinburgh.

At 10 a.m. that grey Wednesday morning he had been shown into an impressive boardroom. Pinewood flooring, walnut wall panelling and impressive portraits of great men lining the walls. Alex Diack should have been awed. But in fact he thrust out his chin and kept his cool.

The gray-haired man in the center of three inquisitors began.

"What makes you think," Gray Hair said, "that we should have anything to do with you at all? That you would be a right and proper employee of this prestigious company, Mister …" and he glanced down at the paper in front of him, seemingly to refresh his memory, "Mister Diack?"

It was no doubt the glance down at the paper that had set Diack off, I would think from what I was to learn of Diack later.

Diack had anticipated the question and came back at him like an express train.

"I'm young, sir, and have no great school education. But life has taught me the hard road and I am willing to give my entire time, energy, and willingness to learn in this company, the sole one I have sought an interview for."

I would bet, I remember thinking to myself, I'd bet that would get them sit up and take notice, these gentlemen of the board of *Melville Erskine*.

Diack continued.

"I know that my determination and my ability to go wherever you send me will give me a good foundation for anything you may ask me."

"So help you God," Gray hair said automatically and smiled.

Alex Diack relaxed. The beginning was over.

The gentleman on the left now began his questioning, describing in general how dispersed and far flung the company's construction sites were, how demanding the conditions were and describing in no uncertain terms the general harshness of life in these places.

Diack said little, sitting bolt upright in the hard wooden chair, his only pair of black shoes pressed tight together, his cap in his hands and his hands gripping his knees tightly.

Finally, Diack told me, it was the time of the third man, who spoke about money, about wages and what he called digs. Diack came to understand that by digs this third man meant lodgings.

After some 45 minutes Diack was asked to leave the room. Blew it, Diack told me.

To his horror and delight there were no other jobseekers in the waiting room outside. Horror perhaps because the job was so difficult that no single other person had applied. Delight because that's meant that as the sole applicant he at least stood a chance. Maybe.

15 minutes later he was called back into the room.

He could tell nothing from the faces of the men behind

the big boardroom table.

But again it was Gray Hair who began.

"You may not be the man we are looking for," he fluffed a handkerchief across his nose and mouth, "but my associates and I are willing to give you a chance. Just a chance, you understand. We need you to make your way to the city of Sheffield, England and report there to our head office. The lady at the desk outside will provide you with a rail chit and five pounds in expenses. You will report at eight o'clock in Sheffield on Friday. The secretary will also apprise you of your wages and terms of conditions. Read them outside in the hall and if you decline to take them up simply hand them back to the secretary."

Diack nodded, thanked the three gentleman and left the room.

In Sheffield, Diack told me, he worked every hour there was on the construction site. He took every opportunity that came his way, shirked nothing, and rapidly gained the respect of both the management and workers on the construction site.

18 months later he was interviewed once more in that same Edinburgh office, by the same three men, who looked as if they had never left the place, and reminded that he had said at his initial interview that he would be prepared to go anywhere for the sake of the company.

CHAPTER TWELVE

We had walked three holes by this time, and to my embarrassment I had paid dad little attention, so engrossed had I become in this man Diack's life story.

Diack had arrived at Kai Tak Airport in Hong Kong in October of 1987.
Melville Erskine had immediately put him to work on the various engineering and roadwork contracts in the New Territories.
Though he was a gweilo, a European, a white face, and was consequently given a fair amount of respect by the Chinese workers, he was nevertheless put to work on site and not in any of the company offices.
Once more he had learned his trade and gained respect for his ability in the hard school of daily tasks on the worksites.
In fact he learned more than that. Saving every dollar he

could, he became aware of stocks and shares.

In October of 1987 the stock market collapsed, Hong Kong shares then plunging 508 points. So Diack kept what money he had safely in an account with the *Hong Kong and Shanghai Bank*. Had he been inclined to put his money into shares he reckoned the only ones to trust would be the *Hong Kong and Shanghai Bank* and *Hong Kong Docks*. If these two failed then everything else would have failed also.

In 1984 the exodus to the United States began. Hong Kong was unashamed in its desire for wealth, and if the colony was going to revert to China in 1997 then the inhabitants were going to make every dollar they could, save every dollar they could, and get out as soon as they could.

Diack shared many of these opinions and began more and more to look towards the future. He began to prepare.

In January of 1988 he began to take flying lessons at the *Hong Kong Aero Club* at Kai Tak, using some of his financial resources. He put the money to good use, taking his PPL in November of that year. Flying out a major Airport such as Kai Tak, he gained an interest in jets and determined to convert to multi engine flying and then jets.

At the same time his interest grew in a young Chinese woman, who was cashier at the company office on site. Her beauty and intelligence attracted him. She was sharp as a tack. He courted her and to the two were married within the year.

I remember Diack stopping suddenly and smiling away

across the water at that point. I can still remember that scene today.

Anyway, in 1989 Alex Diack took the huge decision to leave *Melville Erskine* and start up on his own, his wife Alya Wei becoming his company secretary.

He, or rather he and Alya now that he thought of it, bought a dump truck. A huge, old bulbous, yellow and scarred *Hino*.

Driving it himself, Diack ferried soil from *Melville Erskine* construction sites to wherever else the soil was needed. He drove all the hours God gave, 7/7 where need be. 7 a.m. to 10 p.m. 365.

His wife kept the books, worked her connections and in time suggested he buy another truck.

When he asked her how this could be done she told him her relatives would pitch in. For a small profit of course. And one of her nephews would of course drive the truck.

After 10 months, at Alya Wei's insistence, Diack approached *HSBC*, put his case for a loan and bought himself four more trucks.

Paying off the loan Diack continued to thrive, as did the profits to his *HSBC* business account. He continued to both drive his trucks when he could and supervise the business. With his foresight and determination coupled with Alya May's shrewdness the company flourished, especially during the building boom of those years.

In time he came to own 20 trucks and a burgeoning business.

Diack and Alya carefully bought shares in *HSBC* and *Hong Kong Docks*. If these companies issued share dividends the pair took them, never selling, always adding to both their bank accounts and the shares. Alya's cousin Sam Wei became a close friend and then partner of Diack, an ally he would come to trust more and more as the months went by.

In 1991 all three of them emigrated from Hong Kong to San Francisco and from there moved a year later to Boston Massachusetts.

On the East Coast they used their money and connections to build up a new company called *Diack Technologies*.

Using the same principles of sheer hard work, shrewdness, long days and lack of self pity they built up this new company.

Again I watched Diack's face and saw him smile once more at the memories of those first days in America, the Land of the Free.

At the same time Diack continued his flying lessons and was soon flying a leased twin engined company jet.

In the fall of 99 Alya Wei died as the result of a car accident.

Diack grieved deeply, bitterly then plunged himself back into work. He did not remarry. Alya's cousin Sam Wei remained with him, an ever present friend.

As the years passed, luck favoured him and *Diack Technologies* spun off work to smaller companies and made several affiliates. The company however largely kept these at arm's length and where they failed to meet with Diack's expectations they were immediately set aside. Diack was known for his ruthlessness and efficiency.

Then came the fall of 2008 and its horrendous financial crash.

Though Diack had seen it coming and ring fenced and secured his finances, his company was nevertheless severely jolted by the financial crisis. Other firms crashed totally, bank loans and finances were tight and *Diack Technologies* barely hung on. In fact, as I discovered online on my cellphone, almost half the company's net value was lost.

Ruthlessly Diack pared away the dead wood around him, closing contracts, laying off employees and partner companies with no other thought but to cut costs and keep his head above water. Diack survived but was left with only a portion of his assets and huge loans, though the company remained solvent. Sam Wei stood by him. Diack was enraged at what had happened, enraged but not allowing himself to fall into self pity or a sea of complaints. His Scottish Presbyterian upbringing, his hard education in the school of life and work, together with the business acumen he had gained from Alya and in Hong Kong kept him going. He allowed himself no pity for others, scorned and disregarded the welfare state and any handouts other than essential loans, and believed each person should stand on his own two feet or go under.

Despite his huge losses he shored up his own company, checked his own cash reserves and in a cold rage sat down and made up a plan of revenge.

Revenge on those who had so needlessly diminished his wealth and his future prospects by their greed and stupidity.

He evolved a plan. A recovery plan. A daring and ambitious plan to use not his company resources but his own financial nest egg to recover his future.

This was based on cold calculated planning, a calculated gamble and a vision of the future where his company would once again flourish and he would once more recover the wealth and the lifestyle he and his dear departed Alya May had lost.

At the end of our walk of the outward holes I had almost forgotten all about our family troubles.

Alex Diack turned with me and we began to follow the red flags that indicated the inward nine.

And then, to our greatest pleasure, and obviously to Diack's, the sun appeared, the rain vanished and the estuary of the river Eden glittered with light, as did the wings of several aircraft parked on the tarmac of the RAF base at Leuchars across the river.

"My Learjet's across there," he told me proudly, pointing across the river to the private aircraft on a hard stand at Leuchars.

"I think of myself as a businessman yet really I'm a gambling man. Have been all my life. Look, you can see my jet. It's just taking off now, back to Edinburgh Airport as I asked. Amazing what money does when you have it."

"And how grim the lack of it makes it for you in this life," he added quickly. And for a moment I thought I saw a different man behind the confident, brash exterior. After a moment however Diack smiled again.

"I'm a hell of a gambler though. October last year I

placed bets with a partner of mine at odds of 520 to 1. $30,000 US worth. 5 bets of $6000 each with different bookies. What a chance to take!"

I did the math and silently agreed with him. If he blew it, he really was going to blow it. In style.

But Diack quickly continued.

"Still, it'll help me and my company recover from the worst bloody recession I've ever known, I think. A recession that's just about ruined me. And everybody around me."

That darker face of his again. The realist at heart, I thought.

Then he laughed. The boy at heart, I thought.

"May still ruin me yet. A recession that still makes me burn with anger against those buggers that caused it. Excuse me m'am. May I call you Amy? Good, Amy it is. Yes those evil, greedy, foolish men who nearly made me bankrupt, and many thousands more bankrupt with me. And what had we done to deserve that?

But I've kept my cool, made my plans, cut my losses, used my hoarded, rainy day savings and have set out to get my revenge, as I'm doing now. Plans for a great deal of money with just a little thought, a little planning, and great attention to detail, you see."

I looked up at him as we turned and started on the inward nine. He seemed so sure of himself, this Alex Diack, so cocky, so persuasive. And what plan could he have anyway? And how could anyone be so sure as to bet on the winner of the British Open, as we foreigners call it, and so far in advance?

CHAPTER THIRTEEN

We walked some more, and then I confess I began to pay more attention to Diack's story than to dad's golf and George Orr's caddying.

"In some ways," Diack repeated, "I've always gambled. Gambled on life, on jobs, on my marriage, and on golf. When my father died, when I was only 14 in 1977, I took a chance, perhaps my first chance. I could have stayed on but I gambled and left school at the age of 15 and applied for a job in Edinburgh with that roadworks and engineering company, *Melville Erskine*

He grinned. "Boy was I available! I took a chance on anything that came my way. I moved around a lot, on various construction sites.

I gambled for the second time, big time, when the company asked for volunteers to work in their expanding construction business in Hong Kong. The deal was a three-year contract, a big slice out of my life but with fool travel, board and lodging all found. But that was it. I knew nobody in Hong Kong. Could have been going to perdition and kingdom come."

Diack laughed at the memory of it. "I went out on a limb that time and then again once more when I eventually broke away from the company and founded my own. Then when I married a local girl, Alya. Treble folly, I thought to myself at the time, branching out on my own, marrying and marrying a foreigner!"

Diack tossed his head and laughed out loud again. "Madness! But then to win you have to be a little mad, a little bit daring."

As I looked at him, I felt I had to agree, at least in part.

"Yeah, all of these moves, one whale of a gamble! But I stuck in and succeeded and

Alya and I took the decision to move the fledgling company we'd created and made the dynamic leap to America, land of the free. With a Chinese guy, a relative, a true friend of hers and soon to be mine too.

He stopped for a moment, and mused. "Yeah. The U S of A. Land of the bold and of outrageous money. If you plan well, think hard and are prepared to work yourself to death almost, 15 hours a day, 7 days a week. No holidays. Boy did I suffer! Did we all three suffer!

Our company, I considered it to be mine and Alya's, we built up. *Diack Technologies*, and boy did it expand and diversify!"

Then Diack suddenly sobered, his face became gloomy and a little less confident, just as I had seen earlier.

"Then it all went wrong as I said." Diack looked down and kicked the ground.

Wouldn't have come out of it if it hadn't been for my buddy, my other partner."

Diack looked direct at me. And looking back on things now, I wish for my sake and my mom's, I'd paid more attention to Diack's remark about his buddy, his other partner. It would have made things easier for us later on that week.

Once again Diack had stopped, looking up and gazing away out far over the fairways and greens before talking again.

"But eventually I recovered, in a way, Diack mused. "I suddenly feel free, heedless, reckless almost. Free to let rip, take a real chance and challenge the world any way any way I want. Answerable to nobody, damn them, damn them all!

Odd time to take risks, in an economic downturn. Funny names they called it. The worst in decades so they said. A fiscal collapse they said, those bloody unfeeling masters of words. A full-blown plunge into the abyss.

So once again, more in a deathless fury than anything else I've taken the gambler's way out." Diack smashed his fists together.

I reckon there are thirty top world golfers who competed in the U.S. Open. 30 that are here again in the British Open.

The first golfer I've had my eyes on for over nine months now is that amateur rookie from Pebble Beach, Ritchie McAvon. Know him? Rangy young fellow of 23. I studied him. He haunted the golf courses of California from the age of 10. A raw beginner in some ways and an outsider, especially at 520 to one, as he was last October when I placed a mighty bet on him to win the British Open.

You see, McAvon has mastered those impossible, unpredictable winds gusting off the Pacific at Pebble Beach. You been there?" I shook my head.

"Faced ocean winds that bite straight into your face. He's mastered the need for perfect driving accuracy and narrow line consistency with any club in the bag, but especially the driver. Ritchie McAvon knows from bitter experience that if you miss-hit to the left you can end up in the Pacific Ocean. Flake it to the right and you give yourself very little chance of even making par.

Yes sir! God knows, I've done it often enough myself, in my own stupid amateurish way. Hooked it, sliced it, plain made a hash of it.

But McAvon, you see, has read and learned his home course on the Monterey peninsula and has twice finished high in the California state championship now. He has followed from dawn to dusk the top players who have run the gauntlet of the Pebble Beach golf links.

His father ordered and dictated his life from the age of three. Three, would you believe! That's dedication. Or madness. Bit of me in him then! Had a small set of golf clubs made for the boy at the age of 6, and repeatedly drummed into his son that he would be a greater golfer than his father, the greatest golfer the world would ever see.

That boy, and now the man has breathed in those words of his father and has begun to live his destiny. Especially in the 100th US open at Pebble Beach in 2000. Ritchie McAvon marvelled and followed with a borrowed camcorder Tiger Wood's first round score of 65 there at Pebble and then Tiger's colossal, error-free final Sunday round of 67 for an overall incredible total of 272. Doesn't that bite your butt! Pardon me, Amy. McAvon filmed it all. Played it over and over again on his video, followed and marvelled and learned. Boy did he learn! Hot damn! Now that boy's climbing his way to the top of the ladder and grabbed at that invitation to participate in this championship Open here at St. Andrews, home of golf, yes sir!

So the rookie from Pebble Beach has become much more than a possible, more even than a probable. Someone worth gambling on, I reckoned. Even in spite of the other top golfers, your dad included of course. John Millar Granger."

I looked Diack in the eyes there. Not many people know my dad's full name. He's usually either 'Jack' or 'Granger'.

Surprisingly Diack stopped there, saying not a word. Stood watching dad chip onto the 17th. After a minute, Diack walked on and began speaking again. Irrepressible, Diack seemed.

"Jack Granger, with that caddy George Orr, is good, damned good. Yet maybe not so good I think. True, your dad has won two back-to-back British Opens, five years ago, winning in real fine style.

But that was then and this is now, five years on. He's had two. How can anyone carry off three Open Championships in six, years? Unlikely, my gambling brain tells me.

So my spare money, a huge stash of it, but not my rainy day gold stash, is on McAvon. Despite the debts I have, the money my company still owes. And through that boy McAvon and his coming triumph in this championship now, my lost wealth, so damn profligately squandered and stolen by others, through the foolish consequences of those damned greedy bankers and speculators, will be restored. Yes, restored."

The intensity of the man had to be seen to be believed.

And yet, as we walked, I noticed Diack had scrutinised each green and fairway, and I wondered what his fortunes would be over the next four days of the actual Open that was approaching.

When we reached the 17th green I half watched dad but also Diack as he took obvious pleasure in watching the sand martins swoop and skim over the smooth surface around the pin. What grace and beauty they display, I thought to myself. What simplicity of life and freedom from care. And again I saw this strange mixture of a man, Alex Diack, smile to himself.

Diack rolled up his umbrella and took off the cloth cap he had worn. Now the July sunshine shone on his bald head, his broad features and the breadth of his forty plus year-old shoulders and stocky frame.

He had flashed around the money he had kept, kept up appearances I suppose, signs of wealth and opulence, for he knew that in this world appearances, reputation, counted for everything. But he was also gambling, a little recklessly it seemed to me, on a huge outcome, one that was not wholly or even partly in his control, I thought. Who did I wish to win? My dad, soulless without his darling Laura? Or Diack, also soulless without his wife, and somehow desperate, rudderless in life. But ruthless, I thought.

CHAPTER FOURTEEN

What Alex Diack didn't tell me, and what I wouldn't know till much, much later I wish I had known then.

I watched his face we came to the rise on the 17th green and there spread out before us the old skyline of St Andrews and in the distance the high tower of St Rule.

But, had I known it, it was the view out to our left, the view of the fabled West Sands and the waters of St. Andrews Bay that held Diack's inward thoughts and his immediate past.

Diack had excused himself, abruptly but politely and left me to walk on by himself, while I in some confusion stole a quick look at him, then continued on up to the 18th after dad.

No way to compare this with my home, beautiful though this is, Diack was musing to himself.

His "home", as I later found online on my iPhone and from the realty agent who'd shown him round, was his small private island some miles to the northeast of Bermuda.

Diack had found the place just eleven months before, when the recession was beginning to bite and banks and realty managers were looking for quick cash and ready sales.

He had flown his own private jet from Boston Logan to Bermuda International. From there a charter helicopter had taken the realty manager and him around six different residential properties in Warwick and St. George's.

Until finally the manager had suggested this island with its own waterfront deep channel bulk in the moorings just a hop, as he called it to the north. The same one in fact, that Greg and I rented many months later for our honeymoon from the same realty manager Diack had used. Yes, honeymoon. The boy did me proud in the end!

Anyway, the helicopter had set Diack and the realty manager down on the lawn of a stunningly beautiful residential lot set in 2 1/2 acres. On an island otherwise uninhabited, but with its own helipad, tennis court, unbelievable sea views and five moorings beside its private dock.

Just before Diack had left me at the 17th, I had watched him smile to himself as he turned from the North Sea view before him and no doubt reminisced again about that Caribbean haven he had found.

He must have been captured by it from the moment he

stepped from the realty manager's helicopter, the realty guy told me when Greg and I went to view it initially.

Near the top of the hill amid pine trees and surrounding hibiscus gardens stood a pearl white villa that overlooked the harbour below and two miles of beach frontage.

Totally renovated just ten months previously, the mansion was entered through a central cedar arched doorway into an astounding, lightsome living room. A custom-built cedar bar was tucked into one corner on Diack's immediate left.

Before him an extensive rosewood floor stretched to enormous panoramic windows opening onto the terrace. Away to the far right, sliding doors gave onto a spacious dining room, again lined with broad windows leading to yet another terrace and views of the gardens to the southwest.

This main building also boasted eight bedrooms, all ensuite with views from each of the sea on one side and the gardens on the other. Steps from the two terraces led down to a huge kidney shaped swimming pool and exercise room, with a small wet bar and kitchenette to the west framed by banyan and palm trees.

To the west of the main mansion was a stand-alone guest cottage or studio house with its own pool and terrace. In the main building the master suite and its adjoining office gave Diack a privacy and peace he had rarely enjoyed before.

The whole complex was ring fenced or walled with state of the art security cameras and gate system and tended by a staff of five who lived in the bungalows down round the back of the hill.

Diack must have instantly fallen in love with the place. He snapped it up a mortgage at 10% below the place's bargain offer price and promptly named it *Alya* in honour of his dearly missed wife.

Yes, he no doubt thought as he turned away from the 18th fairway along Granny Clark's Wynd , then back to the St. Andrews Old Course Hotel, life was sweet. And was to become sweeter still.

Diack had been ravished, revitalised by that place. Like a young man again with a brand new cherry red Porsche. From a distance as I walked on, I thought I saw Diack smile to himself again.

Only one problem lay still on his mind, as I know now. That man Jack Granger. The other golf contenders would be easier to dissuade, Diack was thinking But not Granger. And that was why Diack had taken much stronger measures with him, as I discovered.

At his hotel room window Alex Diack now sat, though I didn't know and couldn't see him, watching as the group that included Jack Granger finished off and walked away. Myself, Amy, among them.

On the broad table at which Diack sat lay a copy of the *Times*, open at the order of play and tee-off times for the following four days. Beside that was a lovely pair of Leitz binoculars that Diack used from time to time to check on his *assets*, as he called them, on and around the course and which I only heard about later. Too late as it turned out.

CHAPTER FIFTEEN

Laura, dad's wife and my mom, was being held prisoner in a top floor attic room, as I found out to my cost later. When she awoke that same Wednesday morning mom had had no idea of the time.

Whether it was early-morning about 6 a.m. or later, 8 a.m. she did not know. There was only one window, as I found, boarded up and giving almost no light in the attic room. Only the smallest of gaps appeared at the bottom of two wooden boards screwed down across the window, a gap that gave her only a glimpse of green grass, a grey sea and a sliver of sky above.

She looked round the room. There was almost nothing to be seen. There was the double bed on which she lay, and against one wall a small wash hand basin. A small fireplace with a stool beside it. No wardrobe, no clock, no table, no mirror. Only one single chair to which she had earlier been bound and made the cellphone video sent to dad.

A thick nondescript carpet on the floor. An ancient commode that served her toilet needs, and a horrid roll of toilet paper beside it.

That had been the room she had woken up in for the past five days.

In a few minutes, or perhaps an hour, she did not know, there would come a knock on the door. A key would turn in the lock, the door would open, and two men, but more often just one, would come in.

Faces masked, they or he never spoke to each other or her, simply delivered her a meal on a tray, a meal that, she had learned, had to last her all day. A meal that in the first two days, she ate on her bed as they waited then taped a gag over her mouth and strapped her down on the bed before leaving.

After these first days, they no longer tied her down, or waited while she ate but would leave and the door would be locked as before.

What got her was the silence, the utter noiselessness of the room and the feeling of hopelessness, confusion and loneliness. She felt deserted, forgotten by the world. Her spirit felt as if it was slowly dying, and she with it. And no one would ever know.

And so the day would pass, one day like the next and she was not even sure now which day it was or really how long she had been there, or where she was.

Yet one thing she knew, that she missed her husband and

me, Amy.

And yes, one other thing she knew. She must try to build up hope and somehow or other attract attention. Escape this place, though the odds against it seemed awful.

As usual the man came in and brought her meal on a tray, she told me.

Her thoughts must have tortured her.

"I have tried talking to him but he never answers, never lets me know who he is or what I am. He's Chinese by his features and maybe American but I don't know. And always the mask.

But this morning I somehow get him to stay and listen to me as I ramble on. When I say ramble that's about all I do because I think they've got me half drugged and I still feel dozy and as low as I can possibly get.

This morning I talk about that night in Boston when I went out in my sneakers, jogging suit and silk neck scarf as usual. It was about seven in the evening I suppose, but I still can't quite remember, a cool evening anyway and I was enjoying my run around, when about a mile from the house a dark blue off-road truck pulled up at the curb just a few yards in front of me and a man got out, the very same man I think who is sitting in front of me now, but it's hard to tell. He pulled a knife on me, threatened me and forced me to get into the front passenger seat

He pulled a plastic clip round my wrists, another on my ankles and kept that knife handy pointing at me. Then drove off.

Never said a word, not a word the whole time.

So now I'm in this room, another room from that one I was first put into so long ago, though I have no idea where that was either.

I can ask him questions now and again as I did in the dark blue off-roader and in the first room they took me to, but it still makes no difference. I don't know him really, know nothing about him and I haven't the slightest idea what is to become of me. How dramatic that sounds. But you try several days of this and see how your self confidence frays at the edges then al but disappears. And he has taken care to say nothing, do nothing that will give him or anyone else away.

Since I first set eyes on him he has given nothing away, never spoken a word, never given me any hint or hope.

I might be on the moon for all I know.

I was only aware after a while of being forced way back to write a letter to Jack Granger, my dear husband Jack, explaining that I had left him and giving him some false reasons why.

I assumed this man took my letter and posted it to Jack. Good lord how it must have hurt you Jack, but I had little or no choice.

That seems so long ago now and I miss my Jack and my daughter too, my Amy. Even her partner Greg (sorry Greg!) who I don't really know but was getting to like a bit better each day. But that was before and now I'm here, wherever here is.

I know fine that whatever I say out loud in this room I'm just speaking to myself and I suppose to a world I can't really see. I know that none of that makes a damn bit of difference. I know my tears and my pleas will have no effect, and that you my Chinese friend, whoever you may be, are the only contact I've had for all those days and weeks. How long I don't know. I know you'll just wait there and stare at me, impassive.

I've got no memory really of the darkened room you first put me in all that time ago when I was first taken. I just remember that letter to Jack, then being dragged out of that room, that first room and taken in some vehicle or other, may have been that 4x4, really don't know, taken to a plane, half drugged, half conscious only and hustled aboard a private jet, I think.

But apart from you, I think I've never been aware of another living soul and have been half dopey most of the time, like now.

And in that plane I can dimly remember getting another jab and being made to lie down inside what I thought was a kind of coffin at the time, but which I think now was probably a long box seat in the lounge of an executive jet. But it probably was faked in, as part of the interior of the fuselage.

Anyway I can't really remember it all. It was pleasant enough and whatever mattress or padded bottom I was lying on was ok, leastways I must've fallen asleep again. Next thing I knew I woke up in another dark room, this room, high up in some kind of house I think.

The door is always locked. There's nothing much but a large bed in the room, the window is shuttered, and the only thing I can sometimes hear is seagulls calling and screeching to one another. So must be somewhere by the sea, I suppose.

Oh, and I've searched round the room in my more lucid moments and found only the narrow open chimney place. And there's nothing under the bed but a long plastic curtain rail which is no good to anyone as there's no curtain and the shutters over the window are screwed tight shut.

I might use the curtain rail though, but I need a way to use it that will attract attention. And there's only one way I can think of doing that, shame on me. But we'll see. And that's for later. A last resort. But I must try it. I've had no other constant visitors or minders really.

Just you, my friend and you say nothing, with your food tray every day and a flask of coffee that I suppose must be slightly drugged, for I sleep or doze a lot and can hardly tell whether it's night or day.

I kept my jogging suit and sneakers and the red sweat neckerchief, and you got me two changes of clothing, same as the first lot of jogging clothes I had, and you've let me keep the red silk sweat neckerchief I had on those many days ago when I went jogging and life was simpler and much to be enjoyed, as I know now.

The red neckerchief, maybe. But all in all the other thing would be better, if I dare to use it.

Anyway I'm glad we had this exchange of thoughts, if that's what it is and that you stayed a bit today and listened to me ramble on, whether I talked out loud or just thought these things in my head. It seems to have made no difference to you and almost none to me.

How many weeks and days has it been? Where am I?

Why am I being kept like this? Is it to influence Jack in some way? And why oh why did you get me to write that horrible letter to Jack? And that awful video you concocted yesterday. Must have terrified Jack out of his mind. And Amy too.

But now the Chinese man has got up and left me, locking the door behind him as always. And another day, if it is a day, will come and go.

Even later when my mother told me all this, I could still feel her anguish, her hopelessness.

CHAPTER SIXTEEN

When I got back to the hotel, I met up with Alex Diack again, at a table in the upstairs lounge. That's a really lovely place, with a fantastic view out over the Old Course

Diack's talk was all golf. He apologised for that but there was really no need. I was used to listening to golf talk and Diack was a good talker. I didn't have to say a word, just sit, nod occasionally and generally listen.

Diack talked again about Pebble Beach .

"You know, Pebble Beach Golf Links is the best course on the West Coast and maybe in the whole damn U.S.

Diack was winding up.

"It's got a fantastic view over the Pacific from the Monterey Peninsula."

He slapped the table and nearly spilled the coffee he was toying with.

"And if Pebble's not enough for you then there's Cypress Point Golf Club and then Spyglass Hill Golf resort.

Amateurs designed Pebble. Jack Neville and Douglas Grant. Designed it in 1919 for that far sighted man, Samuel Morse. Jack Neville was a great golfer and won the Californian State Championship twice. Twice! Can you imagine it! The final bill for Pebble's construction was $100,000,they say, and the guys who dreamed her up supposedly based it on a kinda consortium of British links courses. Jack Neville certainly lived and breathed golf.

Pebble was constructed on about 18,000 acres that included the course and the Lodge at Pebble Beach. It held its first major championship in 1929 when it hosted the USGA Amateur Championships. What a time that must have been, yes sir!

Have you ever seen Pebble? No? Well you should.

The first few holes lead inland, away from the ocean, so you don't get to see the Pacific till the fourth. Story goes the original owners of the land that would have been the fifth just plain refused to sell. Don't blame them in a way. View's fantastic. So Neville and Grant had to push the course inland a while till they could head back to the ocean for the sixth.

Diack shook his head in sadness and mock disbelief.

In 1997 the Pebble Beach Company that was formed sealed a deal for the 5 acres of land for $9m US, then asked Jack Nicklaus, to redesign things.

Greens 4, 5 and 7 were rebuilt in consultation with Nicklaus and Ed Connor in 1990, in preparation for the

1992 US Open at Pebble Beach.

A new par-three 5th was built spring and summer of 1998.

The Pebble Beach Company team included former US champions, Johnny Miller and Tom Watson in the initial planning stages.

If you can bear with me boring you still more, Amy, there's two great holes you just have to see to believe and play to understand. One of them runs along a 50ft cliff. Cost $3 million and debuted in the US Open of 2000.

Other's the par four 8th. That, I think, is the most outrageous hole in world championship golf. It's about 420 yards and its scary. The fairway runs along a plateau along the ocean edge and you hit out across a ravine. Scared the life outa me when I tried it.

As for the17th and 18th, just don't try them if you can't manage wind and can't drive accurately. Screw up to the left and you're plumb in the water. Anything right and you'll never make the green in two.

Now Rich McAvon can play these in his sleep, he's done it so often. So I reckon he can more than handle anything this Old Course can throw at him here this week. Know what I mean? Your dad's gonna be real up against it, yes sir."

Well thanks a lot, Alex, I remember thinking to myself. And yet now, when I think of his generosity and selflessness to us, that seems mean of me. And anyway, he was to show just how generous he was to us in a few moments time.

CHAPTER SEVENTEEN

At that point, Greg came in, spotted us and joined the party. Dad and George Orr also appeared a few minutes later and sat down too. At this point the coffee seemed to disappear and some martinis, not too many, took over. "No doubt about it, Greg enthused, that Cadillac Escalade is a big machine."

I noticed that Diack for once kept quiet.

Greg carried on, oblivious to all around, it seemed to me and I wondered at the time why he was doing this.

"Got an invite up into the Blimp floating above," he waved an arm towards the sky above the hotel.

"Friend of mine from The Edinburgh Academy's up there, showed me around and we spotted that Escalade in the hotel car park. What a beauty! I googled it on my I-Phone and boy do the specs make great reading."

Greg seemed to be looking at no one in particular, yet still Diack was strangely quiet.

"It's got power to spare, really comfortable and big in

sheer size. Unlike some off roaders the power plant in this model is more than up to the job, a 6.2-liter V8 with over 400 HP! This latest Cadillac Escalade has a fantastic look. It's definitely not a vehicle for those who like to travel incognito! It's very much in your face.

The one outside there in the hotel carpark shouts at you, doesn't it - Look at me I'm a big success!

Greg went on, unaware that I was cringing a bit at his enthusiasm, unaware that Diack had fallen silent, remained silent.

"I had a quick look inside and it's a beauty! fully automatic climate control, massive heated leather seats, Bose sound system, satnav and great multimedia system, even a rear view camera. And outside the whole machine is dripping in bling and dazzling with chrome. Hell, who can afford one of these?

There was an awkward pause, then Alex Diack coughed and said, "It's mine."

Dad and George Orr then got up in the ensuing silence.

"Well," Granger said apologetically, "George and I were just about to head for the practice ground. Have to keep up with things, while we're hot." Greg didn't know where to look.

"Well then!" Diack let out a great gust of a welcome and stretched out a large hand to Granger. "You may not know me but I'm a great fan of yours on the golf course. Name's Alex Diack. A.J.T. Diack. I've flown up specially for the Open and I've truly enjoyed the first day's golf. Lovely round you had, followed you most of the way around. A joy to watch, you and George.

Congratulations to you both!"

Rather taken aback by this hearty and fulsome approach, Granger leaned over and took the proffered hand.

"Well thanks, thank you for so much praise. Most of the time George here has almost as much to do with it as I have. And have you met my daughter Amy and her friend Greg Walsh?"

Greg stood, his hand taken in a crushing grip, then my hand was gently taken and surprisingly kissed, to my slight embarrassment.

"Amy and I are old friends, aren't we Amy. Nice to meet you, George. You too, Greg."

Before any real answer could be given to any of this, Alex Diack had walked round the chairs, taking dad under one arm and Greg by the other and had launched himself into his usual talking mode again, as if nothing had happened.

Diack nodded affably. "When you're hot you're hot. When you're not, you're not. I know the feeling. Businessman myself, so I have to keep on top of it all." Diack laughed good naturedly.

Then on a more serious note he looked straight at dad.

"But all work and all that, you know. In fact I've come across to bother you all and your manager Mark Meekin too, to invite you to an evening off, if you can spare it. I'd like to drive all five of you with me tonight. To an evening at the Perth Races, if I may. In that saucy overdone Cadillac Escalade. If that's ok with you, Greg?"

My darling Greg could find nothing to say to that.

Granger and the others looked slightly taken aback at Diack's hospitality.

Before they could say anything however, Diack had resumed, continuing his jovial, frontal attack style of conversation.

"I know you don't have too much free time, especially on the first two days of an Open, but you would do me a great honour to come and have dinner and drinks with me at Perth Races this evening. Drive you there, drive you straight back. Early evening, no late hours at all, no time at all, no bother at all. Will you come?"

Granger looked at Diack then at me.

"Well that's mighty generous of you, Mr Diack. I'm not sure if we can all make it. I mean, my manger Mark Meekin isn't here yet, and I'm not sure what Amy and Greg had planned for tonight."

He broke off and glanced at me.

To my surprise it was Greg who responded immediately. "Mr Diack, that's really good of you. We'd love to have an evening out, so long as it's an early one, wouldn't we folks?"

With me looking straight back at Greg and that expression of surprise and pleasure on my face, what could Jack Granger do but agree?

He nodded and said "That would be swell, Mr Diack. Sounds like a pleasant evening's entertainment. Just so long as…"

Diack interrupted. "I know, just so long as I have you all back here nice and early, bright and sharp for tomorrow's start. Though I believe you don't tee off till afternoon tomorrow, as you had an early start this morning. That right? And call me Alex, please."

"Right, Alex. We're off at 14.45."

CHAPTER EIGHTEEN

Greg seemed to have fully recovered his self esteem and poise by the time the others had all left and the two of us were by ourselves.

"Amy, remember how we went with Granger to see the body last night?

I nodded.

"Well I couldn't quite remember the place we were taken to. I know we kind of went on a roundabout route. Took us about 10 minutes. That's quite a route for a small place like St. Andrews.

I remember we stopped in the dark just next to a street lamp. When I thought about it this morning, while you went round with Granger, it wasn't quite like the front to a mortuary or whatever. In fact the more I thought about it, the more I seem to recall it might have been at the back of a building. No other buildings around and just a row of high trees behind.

You remember too, how quickly they got us a taxi and before we got in the taxi how they said just immediate relatives allowed? Then they seemed to have second thoughts and a man came to take all three of us before we had any time to figure out where we really were going.

When we got out at last, the same vehicle, taxi or whatever had waited and it brought us straight back here to the hotel. It was the same taxi. I feel sure of that.

This morning I thought about all that and the body in the burn too.

So I went back to the Swilcan burn not far from the hotel here. You can't quite see the Swilcan from here on the ground so I walked round that way, but before that I asked at the Jigger Inn if the boss last night or the bartender had noticed anything, or heard any noises. After all, there must have been the flashing lights of the police patrol car and then the ambulance. And surely they must have heard the siren.

But nobody in the Jigger Inn had seemed to have heard or seen anything Nobody could remember anything unusual even when I mentioned the time it must have happened.

So eventually I left, had a good look round the Swilcan area as best I could, then went to have a word with the hotel staff here. Of course the people at the reception this morning were not the team that had been on the evening before. But nobody had said anything to the others when the teams changed duties.

I also asked about what people, staff or hotel guests might have seen on TV the night before, at the time

Granger watched it. Again none of the guests or staff had mentioned anything unusual or asked any questions about a local murder shown on TV. Nor was the event repeated on the Scottish news, TV or radio. Nor on the national telly either for that matter, as far as I could find out.

You know Amy, it's almost as if the whole incident never happened. As if nobody else saw it. And one other thing. I'm pretty sure that taxi that they got for us, to take us to the morgue, was an Alpha. You know I'm mad about cars, so I noticed. And that Cadillac Escalade I went on about, that was driven here this morning to the hotel car park. That's why I noticed it. It wasn't here when we first arrived. But I did check the licence online. It's American, of course, Massachusetts, and so pretty obviously Diack's. So the whole thing of the body in the burn was a scam."

I nodded, leaned over and gave him a kiss.

"You've been busy, Greg. Thanks for all that. And there was me, just going round the course with dad on his practice round."

"Yes, how did it go?" Greg asked me.

"It went fine. I scraped my left leg a bit going up the steps outside the R&A clubhouse near the first tee, but they got an elastic bandage on it and it's been fine. No trouble at all. And anyway, Alex Diack, whom you've just met and is taking us out to the races later this afternoon, looked after me and walked round with me. Quite a talker and quite a character, that one. There's a whole history to him and he seems a very likeable guy. Did you find out anything else?"

Greg smiled.

"Yes, Amy. I asked around a bit more because I didn't really understand what had gone on. I ended up talking to a guy from the St. John's ambulance people here at the tented village.

I asked about ambulances and things, where a body would be taken to here in St Andrews. He said he assumed a dead body found in the open air here would be taken to the local hospital in St Andrews.

The only other place it might be transferred to, if there was anything suspicious or odd about it would be Ninewells Hospital, across the bridge in Dundee.

I asked if he was sure, he said 90% he thought it would be likely that the body would in fact be taken initially to the hospital here. Ninewells was possible, and perhaps just to be sure I should try there.

So I got in the car and drove across to Ninewells.

Odd thing happened to me as I drove my Audi 3. On the Tay Road Bridge a plain, white panel van drove up fast behind me, closing to about 3 yards. I thought it was going to shunt me up the behind. There were no other vehicles on that lane of the bridge at the time. The van then zoomed out suddenly to overtake but kept just a foot or two from me.

I thought, what a hell of a driver! Nearly forced me into the guard rail to my left. It stayed there for 50 yards or so, then rocketed way ahead of me, speeding like hell. I didn't even get the plate number, and when I reached the Dundee end of the bridge there was no sign of it and nobody really I could ask about it. So I carried on up to Ninewells Hospital.

Just as well I went there rather than just phoned up, because the woman I had to talk to was a bit frosty with me at first, till it turned out it was her break. About 11.30. and she'd been on since 7. That was what she was annoyed at.

So I said I had had nothing to eat myself and could I take her down to the canteen for something. She lightened up a bit at that and we enjoyed the delights of a battered haddock and chips, with a green salad on the side. Believe it or not she wanted a bottle of Iron Bru to go with it, so I had the same as she ordered."

"Nice one Greg," I laughed.

Greg didn't really laugh at all in reply to that. He was in serious mode and that struck me as unusual. So I let him continue. He spoke again right away. No pause, no asides, just straight on with his account.

"It turned out a possible murder victim in St. Andrews might end up in the morgue at Ninewells in actual fact. What's more, since the corpse might then have been moved last night, say between midnight and 3am, it would have been recorded.

The haddock and the iron brew, plus my sparkling personality of course, must have worked wonders, for when we went back to her desk she checked out the entries for that Tuesday night."

I smiled. At last I had now got a bit of light relief out of Greg.

"Yet there was no reception of a body from St. Andrews

at all," he continued. "Not that night, nor even the whole 10 hours from midnight to 10 a.m. Nothing. Nada. Zilch."

I stared at him in surprise.

"I know," Greg continued. That surprised me too and set me thinking, so I drove back to St. Andrews about 1 p.m. and went down to the local hospital here.

Same result. Nothing. No victim, no body and certainly not anyone from the Swilcan Burn last night.

Seemed really strange to me. I asked about the ambulances. The register showed no call out for any vehicle last night. I chanced my luck and had them check from 6 p.m. yesterday up to midday today. Nothing. Curiouser and curiouser."

Greg shrugged.

"But then people are fallible, register entries can be forgotten or whatever.

So I thought what about the police then, and the taxi, because the rest of what I had already investigated looked odd.

So I spoke to the cabbies at the taxi rank. They treated me like an idiot. An Alfa Romeo as a taxi! You must be mad, they said. Nobody in their right mind would use one of those. Vauxhalls, Fords, Skodas, that's what they use. Great value for money, especially as a diesel, and good and easy to service. But an Alpha, great car but far too good for a taxi!

So out went the taxi idea.

Last stop for me was the police station here. I took it careful and slow like. Not every day you stroll into a police station and inquire about a corpse. Anyway I eventually got the station sergeant to take me seriously. He checked the report book, the night book for Tuesday to today. There was no call out for the 12 hours 6 p.m. to 6 a.m., no report of a scene or disturbance, especially near or on the golf course. So what was I talking about? Managed to wriggle my way out of there as apologetically and self abasingly as I could, without raising too many suspicions, I hope.

The desk sergeant did have one recommendation though, before he let me go. Said I should have a word with the security folk at the R&A. The Royal and Ancient. They would perhaps know something about it all.

So I trotted round to the R&A and they put me on to a plainclothes chap called David Bruce. He listened politely, more politely and attentively than anyone else had up to that point. Listened to all my description details and speculations, then gently poured cold water on the lot.

Asked me if anyone else had seen the incident, or the live scene on the TV, or even the ambulance driver. Or had anyone else seen the police cordon being lifted. Pointed out there was no sign at all at the scene the following morning, otherwise the early-morning security patrol would've spotted it. And there were security guys on duty.

But to leave it all with him. He'd have a walk round and make a few inquiries. Took my name and hotel room number and said he'd get back to me. Get back! Haven't heard a dickey bird since.

So that is how is my inquiries have got me. Nowhere. What do you think, Amy?"

I smiled. "I think your English is just wonderful."

CHAPTER NINETEEN

Greg and I retired to our own room on the third floor of the Old Course Hotel, for we had much to think about, it seemed to me.

I used my cellphone to check any e-mail or texts that had come in and make a few replies.

Then the two of us settled down to watch again the copy Greg had made of the dvd dad had recorded on his Vaio the previous night, the shots of the body in the Swilcan.

"Greg, I want you to put your mind to work on this with me. There are a few things I don't understand about dad's recording. And something sticks at the back of my memory too, but I can't recall what. Check it out with me, will you?"

Greg opened his Blackberry, thumbed to his notepad section and nodded.

I looked across at him and began.

"First, the time of this incident with the dead woman started on tv at 23.03, as the recording shows."

Greg agreed.

But I frowned.

"Two questions come to me, Greg. What time actually was that scene at the Swilcan? And was the woman in the burn murdered?"

Greg wrote then replied.

"I'll check 23.03 again. And Granger said the van had the logo *ASIS* on the side, didn't he? I can ask around again and see who else here in the hotel saw the broadcast. And second, we've assumed the woman was murdered."

"Right," I continued. "The ambulance must have taken her somewhere. So I can go again and check on that here. You know, maybe the recorded shots from the blimp might help, if I can persuade the technician up there to help."

Greg looked out the window.

"We could also look around for the taxi that took us to the morgue. Can you remember anything more about that, Greg?"

My boy Greg replied at once.

"The taxi was silver, an Alfa Romeo. Yes, a silver Alfa, with an illuminated TAXI sign on its roof."

"You're sure Greg? An Alfa?

Walsh nodded quickly as he made a note. "Sure I'm sure. The taxis we've seen and used here in the town have been Vauxhalls or Fords. Diesels most of them. But this one was certainly a Alfa. Thought about buying one myself. In these tight times, an Alfa is a good bargain. Fashionable, seems well made, solid, not expensive. So, yes, it was an Alfa Romeo."

"Right. And would it be easy to fit then dismantle a 'TAXI' sign on a car?"

Greg nodded.

"Then lover, can you chase that up and see which firm, if any, did the trip with us. By the way, was it the same taxi brought the three of us back last night, back to the Old Course Hotel?"

"Sure was, Amy. But I can probably double check it downstairs with the doorman, if it's still the same guy on duty."

I nodded then said thoughtfully.

"If we're going to be asking around, would make sense to check again with the police here too. The dvd shows five police officers outside round the cordonned off Swilcan bridge area, then there were two downstairs when we rushed down with dad. That right?"

"Right. But I can check it up to make certain."

I smiled.

"Right lover. You do that. I'll watch the dvd again, the copy we've made, and see what it was that spooked dad."

Greg leaned across and kissed me long and tenderly. No doubt he thought I looked a bit distracted, a bit paler than my usual cheerful, rosy face. And no doubt my eyes too seemed more pensive than he'd seen. But then, he'd only known me six months or so, hardly time to really understand me, yet long enough to propose. Strange how he'd first seen my photograph on my Twitter page, e-mailed me to help out with a case I said I was chasing up, my missing mom, then taken me out to dinner a couple of nights later. Whirlwind, that's what he was, and somehow it made me thing again of Alex Diack. But surely there was no comparison?

I watched Greg as he pocketed his Blackberry, blew me a kiss and went out of the room.

CHAPTER TWENTY

Left to myself, I wandered round our room for a bit, looked out the windows, then had a cappuccino from the room coffee machine.

Things were odd. I could make little sense of it all. And I missed my mom.

I couldn't settle, so in the end I took my pass key and went into dad's room next door.

There on the coffee table lay the letter he's got from mom all those weeks ago, when she first disappeared.

I picked it up, went to the window and after a glance at the green fairways, the sands and the sea outside, I sat down and read it again.

'Darling, I'm sorry I walked out on you the way I did. I just couldn't take it anymore.

I suppose for lots of people it happens like that. One moment you're relatively happy and well off with a lovely home and beautiful grownup daughter. The next your husband is famous, on top of the world, beating everyone else in the game and fortunate to win more often than not.

But fame brings its troubles. You can't even go shopping without being recognized and stopped or followed by gangs of paparazzi.

And I seem farther away from you and our darling daughter that any time in our lives before.

I just can't take it anymore.

So Honey, go on, lead your life. Beat the rest of the guys on the golf course and do well what you know so well.

Don't worry about me. I shall recover eventually. I shall be watching you from a distance and wishing you well, as I did before. Win St. Andrews, don't let us down. Show this to Amy and give her all my love. Greg too of course. I know Amy will back you up and give you the support you need. Just as she seems to have found the right man in Greg. He's a great guy and a reliable man. Again, all my love, all my best wishes go with you. You know that and can count on it.

Your ever loving,

Lora.'

I rubbed my forehead. There was something odd about that letter too, I thought. Something not right. Mom wasn't a quitter. Oh, she and dad had had their ups and downs, and dad had been away a lot with all his golf tournaments and things. But Laura had known all that before she married him. And she was no quitter. She was a tough woman, when it came to it. I'd seen that when we went climbing and I had to rely more than once on her determination and strength on a rock face or a scree slope.

Yes, the letter sounded odd.

And it ended with the wrong signature.

CHAPTER TWENTY ONE

Greg did in fact talk his way up into the blimp, as I found out.

On Saturday of the week before the Open proper began, as Greg found out from the hotel reception and then was allowed by the Blimp technician to review a little bit on the blimp's recorded warm-up sessions from before the BBC broadcasting real began, a van and two men had presented themselves at the Old Course Hotel and said they had previously phoned reception to say they would be coming, free, as part of the media contract for the 3rd floor of the Hotel.

Their van had been parked in side forecourt of the hotel that morning, as the doorman remembered seeing it and as Greg confirmed on that blimp's early tv recording.

So much we could have known but didn't find out till later.

CHAPTER TWENTY TWO

And later that afternoon, as Diack himself confirmed, the trip to the races was arranged. Though later, I as well as dad had cause to think about just how it had all been arranged so quickly. And how Alex Diack had known so much about our group and the workings of the Open. But then, to someone who was in business, had walked the course and obviously knew his way around, why should Diack not know things?

And why should we not take up such a generous offer and spend an evening out? But I did wonder at the time what the point of the invitation was. Was Diack simply out to impress us?

At four that afternoon, all five of us were collected from the Old Course Hotel by Diack's roomy, dark blue left-hand drive Cadillac 4x4 and taken from St Andrews round to Scone and the Perth Races. There was something about the Cadillac that dogged my memory but I could not recall what. My thoughts were interrupted by our arrival at the racecourse.

Even before we had got out and walked away from the Sponsors' car park the influence of Diack's sponsorship kicked in. We each got a Day Member's badge to pin on, together with a complimentary programme and race card.

A steward led our party across the racecourse itself and on to Diack's private Corporate Hospitality Suite in the Dewhurst Stand.

In the suite we joined the twelve other guests Diack had invited and who were already seated at the large window table, glasses of champagne in their hands.

"First race is at 5.40 and the last at 9.10 pm," the head steward informed us when he had seated us and make sure we each had a champagne or soft drink. "The bar is across there," he pointed. "You can each go and choose anything there you wish, when you wish. Be sure to keep on display the yellow shield Racecourse Pass you have each been given.

You can of course just summon the waiter for the continuous buffet and wine on offer tonight. Bets can be placed directly there, and at any time you can leave this suite and take in the atmosphere of the Parade Ring and later we hope, join Mr Diack at the Winners' Enclosure. You'll see these all clearly marked on the Facilities Key Map inside your programme."

The steward turned and faced Diack. "Mr Diack's

company has kindly sponsored tonight's main even, race no. 4, the Diack Gold Cup over a 3-mile 1 furlong circuit."

Dad and I glanced at each other, then looked up to this man who had such wealth and influence.

Yet Diack himself gave no sign that he was in any way proud or affected by the steward's remarks, and with a movement of his hand waved away any sign of embarrassment or honour.

Yet I could not help noticing that the large television screen in the corner of the private suite was showing the logo of *Diack Technologies* at the bottom of the live broadcast of this and other racetracks around the country. "One last thing folks, "the steward announced, "The P.A. vision and sound system will update you and regularly announce results and the runners for each upcoming race, though the TV screen here will also be keeping you informed." He smiled. "I shall be around, so don't hesitate to bring any queries or requests you may have to me and I shall take care of them." He bowed. "Thank you, and enjoy your evening."

But before he went, the steward came to dad and spoke privately to him.

"Mr Granger, if you or any of your Open group wish to place a bet, I would be pleased to help you do that. In particular Mr Diack has asked me to give you a recommendation for you for race 4, and that is *Fortune Player*. The horse is at 4 to 1 and I believe it will have an excellent chance of winning tonight."

Granger nodded and said apologetically," I don't have

much cash with me."

The steward smiled. "If you would like to place a bet sir, you may use cash or of course any credit card."

"Thank you. May I use American Express?"

The steward bowed. "You may indeed Mr Granger. And just use the private tote counter over there." He pointed to a short corridor off to one side of the dining room.

And indeed, after the first course and a good look at the runners and jockeys for all 6 events, I saw dad stroll across to the tote desk in the side corridor and place bets on three races, including a £200 wager on *Fortune Player*.

As I remember it *Fortune Player* finished first and Granger was an impressed and delighted winner. His other two bets failed miserably.

CHAPTER TWENTY THREE

It was obvious that Diack had booked one of the best private suites for his party there.

After we all had a large champagne and had drunk to Diack's health, hospitality and future success, dad and I went out on to the private balcony overlooking the course and found ourselves a quiet corner seat. Below us to our right they had erected a marquee on the grass, between the Stand and the walkway leading to the Parade Ring.

I began a conversation I had been longing to have with dad for weeks, and now seemed the right time for it.

"Dad, how did you and a mom get along? I mean, I was with you both when I was young but then, you know, I kinda went away. Went to nursery school then primary. And that way I was away from both of you for a good part of each day, not to mention later when I was at junior school then high school. You know, I already just realized it lately but we spent less and less time together as a family."

"I know honey," Grainger smiled. "I know. Part of it all was, is, my fault. I got caught up in the golf thing and that took me away, sometimes for days at a time even when I was just playing the U. S. circuit."

He paused then resumed after a minute.

"I got a lift from all that attention you know. I mean, I was good at golf, but the longer it went, the more I began to have confidence in myself. The more regulation I got too. I began to believe I could make it, do something in the game. And then one weekend I won third spot in a tournament and earned myself $2000. 2000! would you believe it! For the first time in my life I had earned us some money from my golf and not just relied on your mom or any part-time job I could get at the golf club."

"I earned a bit of money, then a bit more, bought some better clubs, won some more money at competitions around the States.

Then one week I saw out the first two days in an open competition, at Pebble Beach it was. Didn't make the cut but my ranking rose and boy was I proud when I came home that weekend and told your mom about it. She was proud of me too. She never despised me or my golf. Always believed in me, believed I would make it one day.

"And one day I did. We were down to our last 300 bucks in the bank account and I hadn't really a bean to my name, just what mom had earned as a high school teacher.

"Did I tell you I met her at a high school prom? Yes, well you know how I felt. She was always cleverer than me but let me believe I was the man of the family, the ultimate breadwinner.

"Anyway Amy, came the day I made it through the cut. Imagine it, right through to Sunday afternoon. Never mind I only finished 73rd. I finished. I'd broken into the top hundred.

"I only realize now what it took to do that, but your mom, she knew it right away and made me feel like a king. I brought home 2,900 bucks. 2900! But I'd done something, won something, and got myself a proper ranking.

"After that I got a player's sheet that listed all the meets throughout the States. I wanted to apply for them all, but your mom sat down with me, like a kind of manager really, and we sorted out the ones I should apply to play in, the ones I could afford and weren't too far away.

"I suppose that's when it started. When I started to gain experience and some kind of recognition. It was also then that I began to stay away from home, from you more and more. Though I don't know how else I could have done it.

"I missed you honey, missed you and much of your growing up. I'm sorry. I missed you and your mom. Left all the hard work of a family to your mom, while I, I thought mostly only of myself and my golf.

"I've been selfish. But mom never complained, never pointed it out to me or made me come back.

"In fact in the summer months she and you would follow me around as I played my tournaments. And all of a sudden I started to win consistently. Small things first. With small prize money. But I got the hang of it. How to concentrate, how much to practise. How to live in one small hotel after another. Till I eventually finished number one in a major. More by luck and chance than just ability and concentration, I can tell you! But I won. The money came in. I got a sponsorship. And mom said I should get me a manager. So she and I picked on Mark Meekin. He made a difference, boy did he make a difference! Taught me what to look out for, things to aim for. How to get better sponsorships.

" Then came the week I finished third in the Augusta. From then on I was in. Didn't have to apply so much after that. I was invited. People wanted to have me, wanted to see me compete.

"And so I did.

"And so I was away from mom and you more and more.

"Then I started to travel abroad. Playing in Europe. Sometimes, in the summertime you came with mom and supported me.

"But by then I had to keep at it, all the time. Keep working at it, sharpening my game, bringing in the money."

"Were you ever tempted to fake it, dad?" I asked. "You know, throw a game, let someone else win?"

Dad shrugged. "Was approached once or twice, honey. Nothing big, but boy, you needed money to do everything. And so I was tempted to do this or that. 'Fiddle, diddle' one guy called it.

"But I reckoned if you did that once, then they had you, you'd never be free again. They could use it against you to force you to do it again and again the way they wanted it, all the rest of your life. You'd have the money all right, the good life. But it wouldn't really be your life anymore.

"So I never did, and had to struggle at times to keep going, to pray that one day I'd make it big.

I looked up at him. "And did it happen, dad?"

A slight wind now tugged at the canvas of the marquee below, and dad seemed to look away for a moment, way out to the west across the racecourse

"Yes, it happened. The first time was when I won Pebble Beach. On a windy, rain swept course. Funny thing, the wind and the rain never seemed to worry me too much. I figured everyone of us was up against the same elements, so might as well get on with it and make the best of it.

Amy laughed. "And so you won Augusta and then the British Open in the same year, and you'd made it, and you dad? All those years of doubting and worrying, not much money and not much family life. You made it!"

"Yes. I made it.' And look where it got me. You went off for more studies, just about as far away as could be.

"And then I must have lost Laura, mom. We must have got so far apart she couldn't take it anymore. And that night, in Boston, she just walked out. walked away. Away from our lovely house in Beacon Hill. Away from all the years we'd worked together to get that house, to get that life. Away from me. Away from you, Amy. I just can't figure it out. I would never have believed she would have done that. Never."

And dad's face went dark again and that gloom that I'd seen now several times over the past few days settled on him.

I leaned over, gave him a hug and saw his face light up a little again.

Greg came over and sat with us, as did Mark Meekin.

I got up and wandered off a bit. I guess I needed a bit of air. I looked around the suite and across at the bar. No sign of Diack but most people seemed to be doing as I was. Taking a breather, enjoying the atmosphere and the sheer opulence of the Dehurst Stand's facilities.

I went out of the Dewhurst Stand and stood enjoying the cool Scottish evening. After a minute or two I felt Greg as he came up behind me and put his arms round my waist.

"Darling," Greg gave his boyish smile. "The very sight of you gets me going. It's just you. All you. He held me tighter. "By the way, I've got some news for you. From our head waiter. Diack's sponsorship tonight is his first and last for this racing season, and that's odd, apparently. He usually hosts and funds three in a year, but he's told the club head steward tonight that he's going to hold off for a while now."

"Swell," I said, pecked him on the cheek and broke away. "Give me a few moments to myself, honey. I just had a long chat with dad and I need time to digest it. OK?"

I could see Greg was a little put out, but I went downstairs, out on to the lawn and into the marquee. There was no one else in it at that moment, so I had time to reflect and try and work things out. I wandered across to a chair on the far wall and sat down.

CHAPTER TWENTY FOUR

It was there, after a minute or so, that I heard a voice, two voices as it turned out a moment later. One was Diack's. The other I didn't recognise at the time.

It was Diack I heard speaking first.

"You know what we discussed October last year in the Bermuda Villa? You know I trust you with my life, just as I have trusted you since the day I got to know you. What we're doing is the riskiest thing I've ever tried, and you know I've tried a few risky deals in my time. Okay?"

Alex Diack continued.

"You know how our business in the States is in hock now, all in hock. In a few days if I don't come up with money to cover my business loans and the mortgage on the Bermuda house I'm nearly finished. All those years of my working life and yours down the tubes. Gone."

I could hear in his voice Diack's pent up rage.

"I hate those arrogant, self-righteous fools of bankers and financiers who brought the sky down on our business and on thousands of other businesses around the world. I hate their guts!"

I heard the sound of one fist being thumped into another.

"But I'm not weeping, I'm not rolling over whingeing and giving up. I'm going to get my money back and fight my way up again. You know how I've always kept my rainy day money stashed away. So far I've kept the banks and the loan sharks off my back. I've kept the business out of the red, just. But there's no extra money left now in the purse and by my latest calculations I need a clear 12 million US to keep us afloat and to claw our way back."

"Yes, I know. It's a risk but I'm going to take it and I need your help. "It's one hell of a gamble, I know, but if I don't bet now and make some money then with the economic downturn we've got and got for the next two, three, four years then I'm done for, no matter my fine house, my rented Learjet and my apparently fancy lifestyle. The great journey of my life, from near poverty in Scotland to wealth through 16 hours a day in Hong Kong, to the land of the free here in the US and the American dream, all that is about to go down the tubes and me and you with it Sam. Make no mistake about it."

"We've used six bookmakers. We've placed identical bets, yet not quite so as to raise any suspicions. Six bets of $25,000 each at 200 to one or better." Sam paused, then wrote some more. "Say three at 200 to one, one at

250 to one, may be two at 300 even. Clear six months before. The bookies bit our hands off. On the face of it this is a sucker bet. Would bring us in at least 12 million it came off at all but the odds so far in advance were crazy, hardly worth the bookies thinking about it. They took the bets, all made the same week, but not the same day and spread out, across the US in the Far East and in Europe. You and I placed them, you and I. No one else. No connections."

"And you get 10%."

I sat in the marquee and thought about that. Crazy, yes. Desperate, yes. Possible, maybe.

I heard Diack continue, more enthusiasm in his voice now.

"Just you and me. But before things start for real tomorrow, I need you continue to front up for me, in St. Andrews itself. I'm in the background. I've put up all the money, cash, no checks. I organize the whole rest of the event, you attend to the on-site details. As we agreed all those months ago when we set this thing up in the Bahamas."

"So what with the state of affairs in the States at the moment, the money the firm owes and the way the lenders are acting, looks like *Diack Technologies* might have to go real soon for Chapter 11."

I was startled and was about to get up and walk away from what was obviously a very private conversation, when the other outside the marquee spoke.

"You mean we're going to the wall, nearly bankrupt?"

No answer came to that, but I assumed Diack's response

was 'yes'. I made to get up, but the chair squeaked a little and I froze.

Before I could do anything more, Diack spoke up, his voice a little harsh.

"We're not going to go to the wall, you hear me! We're going to make this work. We're going to collect on this Open Championship. Now listen to me, and let's get this right."

At this moment the breeze made the canvas wall of the marquee billow a bit, and I thought perhaps the two outside would move away, move indoors out of the wind. But Diack's voice continued, quieter now but more determined still.

"You get the PhaSR's lined up. No need to use them till Sunday, though. Only the guys in the 6 pairs going out last on Sunday will be in the reckoning to finish first. So save the laser cameras for them. Got it? Good. We got Granger. No need to try any blackmail or underhand stuff on the others, though we collected the dirt and allegations of bribery on several of them. Just use the PhaSR's, and then only if it's an absolute must, you hear me? Right then, you get back and I'll go mingle, do my PR bit and keep them happy."

When I heard them move off, I jumped up, ran to the marquee entrance and hurried round to the back.

I saw Diack striding off towards the stairs, up towards the box.

Of the other person in the conversation, there was no sign.

When I came back into the restaurant, there was Diack standing by the bar, a glass of coke in his hand. Dad and Greg were standing next to him. All three were laughing, and dad was holding a large envelope in his hand. The tip he had been given had come up and dad was £250 richer.

Seemed everyone was happy. Except me. I couldn't figure it out. What was a phasar, however it was spelled? And how could Diack look and act so happy and at ease when his company was folding around him at this minute? And he was so desperate?

THURSDAY

DATABOARD.

Day: **Thursday. Day 1.**

Weathercast: Wind from South 5-11 mph.
        Overhead   10% cloud.
        Forecast   Clear

BoardWatch: 156 players, 3-grouped.
        First tee off 06.30 BST.
        11min intervals.

Chapter Twenty Six

I stood with dad as he prepared to go from the practice ground to the Starter's Box. Greg had headed off to Leuchars airfield to see if he could get any more information about Diack's Learjet that had departed the day before, and about Diack himself, if he could.

"You know, dad, that was quite some show Alex Diack put on last night, I mean all that corporate hospitality at sponsoring a race at Perth."

"Sure was. He's an influential man, that's for sure and did us proud. Handled well that knock that Mark Meekin took on the head. It was seen to in no time."

Amy nodded. "The auto to Scone, right into the members' car park then the enclosure, the badges that we got, and the obvious deference they paid to him there, not to mention the advert for his company on the race card program. He must be worth a fortune."

"And a nice man, too, "Granger added." Strange I hadn't noticed him before. And yet I get the feeling I have seen him, but heck, I just can't figure out where or when."

"Didn't mum meet him sometime, at a party or something?" Amy asked.

Granger shook his head. "Not that I can remember. But if it was, then it was quite a time ago."

Granger shook out his napkin, folded it looked up at the sky. "Got to go now Amy. Get some shots in on the putting I think this morning. See what happens today. See you on the first tee, darling." He leaned forward to kiss me, then left the breakfast room by the rear door to make his way across past the tented village to the practice green.

26. I checked the Databoard again.

DATABOARD.

Day:	Thursday. Day 1.

Weather Watch:	Slight wind from South West, 3-5 mph.
	Overhead 4% cloud.
	Forecast Clear

BoardWatch:	156 players, 3-grouped.
	First tee off 06.30 BST.
	11min intervals.
	Tee off J. Granger 09.09, Match 15.

So I had to be sure to go round all the way with dad.

Overnight the rain had stopped, I noticed, to be replaced by one of those marvellous Scottish days. A wind that was a mere breeze, barely lifting the flags.

The sky above the Club House, the Starter's Box and the hotels along the Scores was a vivid and serene blue.

I stood as close to dad as I could in the ring of followers, watched and listened as Jack Granger stepped out, past the outstretched hands, the well-wishers, the idle curious, the cameras and the microphones, the whole circus routine of it all, his caddy George Orr at his side, smiling up at him, reassuring as ever. More so perhaps, on this day of all days.

"Jack, got your Sony in the hotel on DVD record like usual so we can study the play later?"

"Yep, George. Say, did you catch that live tv scene at the Swilcan bridge Tuesday night?"

"No Jack. Must have missed it. But you got it recorded on your Sony, right?"

Granger nodded to his caddy, then pointed to the official starter, "Here we go, George."

"Ladies and gentlemen, match number 15. On the tee, from Boston, USA, the 2 times Open holder, Jack Granger!"

Granger tipped the brim of his cap, yet I would bet dad hardly heard the words or the huge applause that followed.

"3 iron, like we said, George?"

"You got it, Jack."

Granger stepped forward, pressed his tee into the green

of the grass, placed the ball, and with little preamble hit his iron shot smack down the middle of the fairway. I felt sure he was more relaxed now he had something to do. To me he almost seemed to be smiling, as if all he had to do now was just concentrate and play.

It had begun.

And yet, as he told me later, dad broke his first rule. He did not concentrate totally on his game. Like every top golfer he was only happiest when he had settled down into his own private world on the course. His own little cocoon. A private bubble, if you wish, where he saw yet concentrated only on his next shot, the next fairway layout already locked into his mind, the configuration of the green and the all important pin position.

But this day, despite himself he thought about his wife, Laura. And he thought about the woman in the Swilcan. What was the relevance of a woman who looked very like Laura? Coincidence? And happened to appear on the eve of this Open Championship now. Coincidence? Both on television and also just outside his hotel? Coincidences? Too many coincidences? And then there was that e-mail to him this morning, on his iPhone.

He regained his concentration again as Orr came up to him, a club in his hand.

CHAPTER TWENTY SEVEN

Meanwhile I had come up the steps in front of the R&A Clubhouse, flipped out my slim cell phone to check my texts. As I did so I also looked up as a movement above me caught my eye.

A man with a cigarette in his mouth and a window wiper in one hand, the same window cleaner I had seen at the start of the week, was standing high on a ladder propped against the front wall of the Royal and Ancient clubhouse overlooking the first tee of the Open.

He was washing the windows, methodically cleaning off with his wipe the cleaning fluid he had spread over the window. Seemed to be taking a long time about it. And looking all round whenever he could.

I noticed him as he watched out of the corner of his eye the man in a tweed jacket sitting reading his copy of the Times in the room on the upper floor. The window cleaner knew this man would rise from time to time and sweep with his binoculars the tee and crowds in front of the clubhouse and away to either side, towards the tented village, the sands and car park in one direction, and in the other to the eighteenth fairway and green, the road, shops, hotels and houses alongside.

It was at that moment I missed my step, stumbled and fell down the stone steps. I had slightly bruised my thigh. No great thing, but annoying. And how embarrassed I felt!

Behind me came a voice, jovial yet somehow stern.

"What have you done there, lass? Are you alright? Here, let me help you up."

It was Peter Graichen, the window cleaner, the man from up on the ladder. Covering my confusion artfully he took me under the arm and helped me to my feet.

"Here, You're Jack Granger's daughter aren't you? Peter Graichen at your service. I know the nurse here in the A&R Clubhouse, so let's go back in and get a bandage on that. It's not too bad, is it?"

And this tall, lean gentleman, ushered me quickly into the R&A, the hallow of hallows I understood, where he organised the resident nurse to clean, patch up and put an elastic bandage on my thigh. I felt a phoney. And I was very much in a man's world there. It was nothing really, I was alright and insisted I must get out there and go round with my dad, Jack Granger, as I explained to this Peter Graichen. But he and the nurse insisted I sit for a while and rest my leg for a moment.

As I said before, you sometimes feel you're not your own

person here. The Open in some ways controls what you do and how you do it. So I sat down by the Clubhouse window, looked out onto the 1st tee and fairway, and sipped my coffee.

The nurse was still fussing around when my cellphone gave a low vibration. I of course had intended to switch it off while on the course, and at this moment it was in silent mode.

I pulled it out of my shoulder bag, held it up and asked nurse if I could use it there in the Clubhouse? She nodded silently but put a finger to her lips and motioned me back into a quiet recess area. I got the message. I could listen or text but no speaking. Fair enough, though I wondered perhaps if the rules about cellphones were the same in the Clubhouse as they were on the course.

It was Greg of course, so I whispered that I could listen but couldn't really speak in the circumstances.

"Lucky they allowed you to use the mobile at all!" he said. Typical Greg.

"Anyway I'll bring you up to date with what they've told me so far here.

Managed to get hold of the flight lieutenant in charge of the private sectoring of the visiting aircraft here this week. He tells me the Learjet arrived Sunday morning, from the States. Apparently this model is capable of such a long hop, or to be safe one quick stopover.

The Flt Lieutenant still had all the specs on his arrivals/departures clipboard that he went and got from the control tower here. This particular machine has a high-speed cruise of Mach 0.82 and a transcontinental range of up to 3,000 nautical miles. Some machine.

By the way the same aircraft, with Diack piloting and a co-pilot accompanying him, landed here just over 4 weeks back. At that time Diack stayed three days, spending the time in St Andrews.

With his co-pilot, a Chinese American, Diack walked the whole of the Old Course, it seems, on the last Sunday the public were still allowed before the whole course was taken over for the pre-Open final preparations.

And again by the way, the log book for the plane records it was also leased at one point by a company called *Brand Avionics*. Now didn't you say the husband of that woman you met at Edinburgh Castle was called Brand or something like that and was also from Boston, nominated the home base for this Learjet?

I know, I know! You can't speak. So tell me later, ok.

Anyway this machine ticks all the boxes.

Rockwell Collins Pro Line Fusion avionics suite, dual automatic Attitude Heading Reference System, or AHRS to those and such as those in the know. Integrated Flight Information System (IFIS) with electronic charts, Terrain Awareness and Warning System (TAWS), can cruise comfortably at 45,000 ft with 31,200 lb cruise weight, and on and on it goes. I won't bore you with the rest of the details, Amy"

I nodded vehemently to myself as I listened silently to this mindless recital of facts and figures, the kind of stuff Greg just loves to pore over, like he did with the specs on the Cadillac Escalade.

"Tell me about the lounge, the passenger area in the

Learjet," I whispered, still afraid of being overheard.

"Well the lounge is sumptuous. Room for 6 easily, all easy chair comfort. There's one roomy bench seat with a coffee type table in front of it. The top layer of the bench comes off and there's a recessed storage space along its length. You know, there's not much room for overhead lockers, so this doubles as a storage space."

Greg stopped and I dared not speak as I heard someone come into the room then move across it and exit by the side door.

Taking my silence for some kind of encouragement or at least passive acceptance, Greg ploughed on remorselessly.

"3000 nautical miles by the way (how I hated Greg's 'by the way' now) is about 3,455 standard miles the geeks here tell me. So a fair range."

But I had been thinking as Greg had ploughed on. And now I couldn't control myself. I leaned down, head under the table I was sitting at, as if to tie a shoe lace, and whispered loud as I dared into my cellphone.

"Got two questions. Was the Learjet customs cleared at Leuchars or someplace else?"

There was a pause for a moment, presumably as Greg conferred with the Flight Lieutenant. Then back came Greg's answer.

"It was cleared here. Last Sunday on arrival. You've got to remember it had visited here already and all its specs were known, so the inspection didn't take too long.

And the second question, Amy?"

I whispered again, hoarsely but loud as I dared.

"Who collected the jet on Wednesday this week and where did it go?"

There was almost no pause this time, as the answer came back right away.

"Flt Lt Rogers says it was signed off and flown to Edinburgh Turnhouse with one of their aircrew reps as co-pilot. Signed off for Air Enhance, can't make out the signature but it is signed off. Not by the crew that flew her in, of course, Amy."

And I thought to myself . Of course not. Diack is still here, for the golf. And so the other one, the co-pilot must also be here. But why? For what purpose?

At that point there was a massive roar, made as Greg told me later, by two RAF Tornados taking off in echelon down the runway and blasting out over the North Sea.

And later, Greg, being Greg, managed to bum his way on to an RAF helicopter that flew him back to St Andrews. While a flight sergeant drove Greg's car back to the hotel here.

Typical Greg.

CHAPTER TWENTY EIGHT

Graichen sat again at the top window of the round tower at the end of Hamilton Hall.

Beside him on the windowsill lay his mobile. His boss, Douglas Bruce, had only phoned once to check up on him that morning and that must be a record, he thought to himself. He was forever worrying, that man. A great worrier, but then Graichen supposed he had a lot to worry about.

As one of the Cleaning Squad around to the Open course at St. Andrews, Graichen's job was to service everything round about the R&A Clubhouse, Hamilton Hall and the houses nearby. That was to say, the Links Road running up the side of the 18th fairway.

As far as Graichen knew, Hamilton Hall was unoccupied

as yet and he was the only person in the whole building. Though the whole place was being refurbished and was looking a treat.

He put out the stub of his cigarette, picked up the carton of coffee he had brought and took a sip.

CHAPTER TWENTY NINE

Caddy George Orr glanced across at his boss and partner, Jack Granger, who was striding off ahead of the others down the 1st fairway.

Orr paid little attention to the other two competitors in the three-ball. They would have to struggle with their thoughts, just as he and Granger did with their own. This was not just a game of golf. It was a championship and much was at stake. And not just a championship either but an Open, at St Andrews. If your mind was not on winning, you may as well not take part, Granger and he had long since decided. So compete they would. And win.

Orr looked on as Jack Granger took the iron he handed him, chipped the green to the 1st and sank a seven-foot putt for a 3.

George Orr grinned at Granger, shouldered the bag, and the two moved on to the second tee.

CHAPTER THIRTY

The round took four and a half hours. Granger carded a 67. After it was over and they had taken a snack in their room with me and Greg, Jack Granger and caddy George Orr went off to the practice ground to work on dad's driving and chips. Both saw these as paramount in future progress in the second round the day after. They were pleased with Granger's first round and first on the leader board, yet McAvon was close behind with a 69, despite the fact that he was new to the course. Both Granger and Orr believed they could do better still on the following day.

Greg and I had retired to our own room on the third floor of the Old Course Hotel, for we too had some things to consider.

Greg had used his HP laptop to check the e-mail on

his freelance reporter's website and respond to some requests there.

On my iPhone I quickly found Air Enhance and discovered they had an office at Edinburgh Turnhouse airport. Interesting, I thought. I also eventually discovered a list of the aircraft they offered for rental. Two of these were Learjets, the latest model. I checked with Greg and for once his megalomania for the facts and figures of planes and cars proved a bonus.

The specs for Air Enhance's new Learjets matched the data that Greg had got from the flight lieutenant at Leuchars that morning. It seemed to prove the plane that had been there was the same as one of their two aircraft. And the fact it had been flown back to Edinburgh was convincing too. So it would definitely be the one rented by Diack as he had said. But I wanted to be absolutely clear in my own mind who the pilot was and there seemed to be no way to find that out.

"Greg, any chance your flight lieutenant could find out who actually flew that Learjet back to Edinburgh yesterday? And something sticks at the back of my memory too, but I can't recall what. Was it an Air Enhance plane that crashed on its way to LA last year?"

Greg flipped out his Blackberry and made a couple of notes in his memopad, then nodded.

"You got it, honey"

I looked across at him and thought his American was getting better.

I watched as he called up the flight lieutenant. After a few seconds Greg turned to me.

"Off duty today but will be back again tomorrow. I've left a call-back tag on his voice mail.

He tapped away a bit more now on his laptop, grunted, then spoke.

"Got the report on that LA crash. Plane is just recorded as being one of *Diack Technologies*' but no other details pending an official air crash investigation and that's not due out till next month, would you believe."

I nodded.

"I believe. They take forever over these things. I sometimes wonder if one reason for the delay is to allow things to cool down a bit in the interval."

"And maybe to get people to forget or become less certain about the facts of the accident and the death of those they loved?" Greg said.

He had a point.

Then he came up with one of those rare flashes of brilliance he's capable of from time to time. That is, if you believe a lawyer can occasionally come up with a rare flash of brilliance.

"Would there be any details though or any connection with the firm that woman you saved on Edinburgh Castle talked about?"

"Greg, I didn't 'save' her. She just stumbled as the one o'clock gun went off. She dropped the ring she was holding. It bounced on the parapet and she lunged forward to get it. I grabbed her, thinking she was about to throw herself over, or fall over, I don't know what. I blocked off the ring with my sleeve and managed to hold onto her. That was all. No saving in it."

"Amy honey, you're too modest. It might not have turned out to be an accident."

Accident. The word Greg had just used was the one the woman had used that day.

'My husband Robert gave it to me before we married. He ran his own avionics company. But he and my son were both killed in an accident, an air crash.'

And the words engraved on the ring had been '*R Brand to Lisa, Boston.*'

My mind raced.

So the name was Robert Brand, and he had owned an avionics company, in Boston, and somehow that company had been connected to Diack, for Robert Brand and his son had been aboard Diack's plane that had crashed near L.A.

An avionics company.

I tapped into my iPhone 'Brand Avionics Boston'.

I could have, should have got Greg to do it, for his laptop was faster online than my cellphone, but I got there.

There were several Brands listed. But only one in Boston. *Brand Avionics*

And there I read the short summary of the now defunct company, *Brand Avionics* and how it had been built up and prospered and probably over-borrowed and then had gone down the tubes in those awful years of the greatest financial collapses since the 30's.

I was sad. It was sad. A woman had lost her husband and her son. For no apparent reason. Just the way things had turned out.

Her husband had lost his company.

And now that woman was alone and to be pitied. Sad.

Still, apart from trying to share some of that woman's sadness, all I could do was think about her, remember her.

She had my cellphone number. I did not have hers.

Greg leaned across and kissed me. No doubt he thought I was chasing up small details for not much advantage, but there was something there I'd overlooked, for sure.

He put away his laptop, put his Blackberry in his jacket pocket, waved to me and went out of the room.

I was left just as puzzled as I had been earlier. Nothing seemed to be resolved, and something still nagged at the back of my memory.

I stood for a while and looked down at the window at the Swilcan burn and its bridge.

"And there's nothing down there now to show anything ever took place," I thought to myself. "But then, they'd want everything tidied up and out of the way for the Thursday morning anyway, wouldn't they? For the first day proper of the Open."

CHAPTER THIRTY ONE

Greg spent the whole of that Thursday afternoon taking advantage of the good nature of the crew of the blimp. Of course he stayed out of their way in the live transmission shots, but at every other moment he prevailed on one of the technicians, Sam Foster, to find for him and then run, the videos of the shots he requested.

High in the blimp the recorded playback view on 1 was from the far out 9th hole back towards the buildings and spires of St Andrews, with the bay off to the left. The playback alternate on Screen 2 was of today's shots, including one of Granger turning onto the home nine. On the Backup Screen Greg set about sifting through the views the camera team had taken early Sunday through Wednesday, some of them practice shots, others cuts for newsreels and whatnot. One shot amazed him. It was from the north end of the course, just above the 9th green and the estuary of the River Eden. The Day/Date insert read Sunday last, and the time as 08.47.

In the background a Learjet was on final approach to land at Leuchars.

FRIDAY

<u>DATABOARD.</u>

Day: **Friday. Day 2.**

Weather   Wind from South West, 10-12 mph
Watch:

	Overhead	15% cloud.
	Forecast	Clear

BoardWatch: 156 players 3-grouped.
First tee off 06.30 BST.
11min intervals.

Previous Day's Scores:

Player	Out	In	Total	Overall	Position
Round 1					
Granger	34	33	67	67	1
McAvon	35	34	69	69	2

CHAPTER THIRTY TWO

It was Friday morning that Granger got the e-mail. Yielding to my insistence dad had ditched the old outdated cell phone he had used for many years and upgraded to a 32 GB iPhone much like mine.

I had made all the arrangements for him, thinking also that it might raise him out of the depression after Laura's disappearance. There had been word in the media about a possible breakdown in their marriage, hints that he had been seen with another woman while on tour. Granger and I however had always denied any rumors of a rift.

After Laura's disappearance I had insisted dad should modernize, take a step forward, but I had reminded Granger also that simply to have an iPhone was not enough. He had to have it by him most, if not all, of the time. And he must use it. If he communicated with no one, no one would communicate with him.

What's more, I made him agree to try all kinds of communications. I knew he enjoyed using his Sony laptop, particularly for recording on the DVD the live sessions the broadcasters' made of his rounds of golf. So that side of things proved no problem.

But I pointed out that the cell phone could achieve so much more in some aspects. And also it could of course bring him into a new world of texts and e-mails, not to mention scanning the web. So he must use all of these functions, I said.

Greg as usual had gone out and about. No doubt up once more in that blimp.

Dad flipped open his cellphone and rolled his finger over the Email button. I knew he had made an effort to do that each day and so as he checked his e-mail that day before he was due to go to the practice area and tee off later, I was not really paying too close attention. One simple looking e-mail appeared onscreen. But looking back on it, that was enough to change his life.

It seemed innocent enough at first glance, simply titled 'Granger Golf.' There was no indication of the sender.

But the first words blew his mind away and he gasped out loud. I leaned over and looked at the screen.

"Like I said before, the body in the burn could have been Laura."

"Make sure to open the two attachments below if you value your wife's life."

There was nothing more, no-name, no clues as to the sender.

Granger clicked to open the first attachment. It was a document, short and sweet. And yet not sweet at all. Mind blowing.

"I still hold your wife. She is well at the moment and viewing your progress in the Open with great attention. But I hold her. She is mine. I will do with her as I will, according to how you perform now on the golf course. This e-mail is sent through a throw away mobile."

I noticed he inadvertently used 'cellphone' earlier but now we had 'mobile'.

"Take a look at the other attachment, a video clip that I am sure will interest you."

Shaken, Granger double clicked the video.

It took a second or two to come through, but the video when it appeared was another simple file. It was clear and obvious enough though.

The scene was an indoors one, much as we had seen before. In it mom was clearly visible, sitting again in the same plain straight-backed wooden chair as before, her wrists and ankles again tied to the arm rests and legs of the chair.

Laura was blindfolded and gagged but her features were clear enough. Without a doubt it was mom. At someone's beckoning the camera moved to show the tattoo of the claret jug just below the back of her neck.

Dad's horror grew as the realization hit him that this was no look-alike from the burn but his own wife. How could anyone do such a thing to a helpless and innocent woman?

Yet it was Laura, dad's wife, my mom, and though

suffering, she was alive, as was proved when a gloved hand reached into the shot and released the gag.

I noticed something briefly on the wrist that appeared above the glove, but the whole thing was so quick that I had no time to really pay attention to it or to react.

Dad and I watched as Laura shook her head in relief and swallowed several times while she tried to regain some composure. It was obvious she had again been warned what to do and say, for when she spoke her words were curt and to the point.

"Hi darling. I'm okay and well. No one has molested me so far. I will be released if you do as he wishes. That is, play well this weekend. But make sure you don't win."

Mom's mouth trembled and she was shaking a little. Then the hand reappeared and this time a hood was drawn down over mom's head.

Again the video stopped and that final shot remained onscreen.

Whoever it was was certainly putting the pressure now on dad. Much more than the time before, it seemed to me.

The rehearsed speech again showed how determined these people were that dad should not win and I wondered about that now. Did this mean that in fact dad was still seen as the likely winner of this Open? Were they, whoever 'they' were, getting more desperate as time went on? And what did they hope to gain out of the whole thing? The only motive I could think of was money. When I asked dad about this, he could think of no other advantage either, unless an agent of one of the other players was fixated on his player winning and so getting a guaranteed and automatic multi-appearance in the Open for the years ahead.

The fact that mom was again shown bound hand and foot to that plain, hard, uncomfortable chair underlined again the idea of compulsion and the anguish mom's imprisonment must be causing her.

I looked up. Dad had almost completely broken down. Tears were falling straight down his cheeks. His shoulders were heaving as he sobbed.

"How long can this go on?" he moaned. "What means more, my golf? Or my wife? They've got me for sure now. I have no choice, do I?"

I did the only thing I could. I grabbed dad by the shoulders and shook him till he came to himself. And that took a while, I can tell you. I was glad Greg wasn't there to see it.

When dad had come out of it a little, I took his face between my hands and put my face close to his so he could see nothing but me. I could hardly get him to look me in the eye.

"Dad, head up. We have a chance. Two chances in fact. Do you hear me?"

I had to say this twice to him till I was sure it had sunk in and he was paying attention.

"What two chances?" he asked me tearfully. "I saw no chances, none at all."

I raised my voice a pitch and came at him.

"We have two chances. The person in the shot made two

mistakes. Two."

Dad was looking straight at me now and perhaps a bit more hopefully.

"First the sender had inadvertently used two different terms. 'Cellphone', and then later, 'mobile'. Does that mean the person is used to American terminology and yet is basically British? So we have someone who's lived in America for a while and recently if not now. And yet is British. Or brought up and probably worked in a British environment."

"And second?"

I nodded.

"Second, there was a tattoo on one wrist. Just caught a glimpse of it, but there was a dragon and a character, a Chinese character I think, set above it."

Dad had slumped in a chair and was again not looking at me, staring morosely out the hotel window.

"How does that help, Amy?"

"I can get a print off that tattoo, bad as the video is, enlarge it and enhance it as best I can on Greg's laptop, or on yours for that matter, then show it to the deputy house manager here in the hotel. He's Chinese but been in the hotel trade here for over 15 years, he was telling me. I think, I hope, he'll be able to decipher it.

"Meanwhile," I continued, "You leave the whole thing to me. Go off and do your practice and confer on strategy with George, as you usually do. And keep your chin up. Do you hear me, dad, love of my life?" And I hugged him and smiled to him till he nodded and went out.

Ten minutes later I had a print of sorts of the guy's wrist

out of Greg's laptop and the HP printer he had with him.
I took it downstairs, managed to get a hold of the deputy
house manager, who took one look at it and said,
"Wei. It's the character for the family Wei."
So the name of the man in the video shot with mom was
Wei. He was Chinese. And if he had an English British
background and upbringing, and this idea was slightly
more of a long shot now, but possible, then he had lived
or been brought up in Singapore.
Or maybe Hong Kong.
And Diack had been in Hong Kong.

SATURDAY

DATABOARD.

Day: **Saturday. Day 3.**

Weather   Wind from South West, 9-10 mph.
Watch:

              Overhead   49% cloud.
              Forecast   Cloudy/Bright.
              Rising wind from South West.

BoardWatch: 68 players 2-grouped.
              First tee off 08.00,
              Last 14.30 BST.
              10min intervals.

Previous Day's Scores:

Player	Out	In	Total	Overall	Position
Round 2					
Granger	36	33	69	136	1
McAvon	34	34	68	137	2

Tee Off: McAvon-Granger   14.20 BST

CHAPTER THIRTY THREE

I sat alone on the balcony of our hotel room, looking out across the Old Course fairways, the West Sands and the blue sea and thinking of all that had happened in the days before this championship.

As I had learned from the web, Diack had mortgaged a house in the Bahamas, in the days when he and his company were flush and at the top of the tree.

How I wish I had been there originally at that house. It was put up for rent again a few weeks after this whole episode, when Greg and I flew down to see just what kind of a place Diack had had, and what must have transpired there a year before.

Standing in that beautiful living room, taking in the view and the house, listening to the same agent that had showed Diack around, and adding in what I'd read online in the papers and about Diack, I knew I could imagine the scene that had taken place there, especially as the agent had described to me Diack's excitement at the arrival of the second man the agent had brought across to the villa by helo that morning in October last year.

The agent had stayed for a drink in the lounge then walked out into the gardens to kill time before taking the visitor back again to the airport an hour or so later. The side door to the veranda stood open, to air the house, and as the agent had stood near it and smoked, he had overheard the men talking. Though he couldn't look up and see, it had been clear to the agent how Diack did most of the talking in the lounge and the visitor did almost all of the listening.

The visitor had sat as Alex Diack paced up and down between his desk and the window of the house. Diack had seemed oblivious to the beauty of the sun on the water outside or the gardens below.

He pointed a finger at the visitor.

"Make no mistake. I am, I was, a wealthy man. But I worked and slaved and took chances to build my company over the last 15 years and to help and encourage 10 other affiliated companies.

I don't own the house you see here. I don't own the island this house is on. I rent it and now I'll terminate the lease because my company must make economies and those economies start with me.

They call this a downturn. The hell it is! They use fancy words. They call for a tightening of belts, for stringent economies and cuts but there is next to nothing to help the companies that have suffered, the individuals whose lives are bloodied, battered and ruined. The banking world, the financial world are not really sorry for what has happened. Even today they don't recognize the need for a real change of the system. Some bonuses paid are equivalent to the lifetime salary of some people who have been made redundant, losing their jobs in the hundreds of thousands, with tens of thousands losing their homes. Bankers and so-called financial experts set off a collapse that ruined the lives of millions throughout the world.

Taxation will have to increase and public services will be reduced to pay for the calamity. We shall pay for it. The next generation and maybe the one after that will pay for it.

The financial system suffered a near death trauma, a severe heart attack.

People with no one to back them up have been brought to their knees, impoverished, living in want, not knowing what the next day will bring. Literally counting the pennies and terrified that there will not be enough to last out to the end of the month.

Diack smashed one fist into another.

"Now you can sit and weep and wail and moan and blame others, give up hope completely. Or you can act. Not sit down and take it. Fight back. Plan and beat them at their own game.

"With a person like you, loyal and absolutely trustworthy, I have worked out an idea.

This is what we are going to do.

The agent had seen Diack paused then come up to the

visitor and place both hands on the visitor's shoulders. Diack had spoken almost in the man's ear, so quietly that the agent was sure the man would have had to strain to hear.

"Much of my money, much of my company's money has gone. I have placed half of what remains in security. The other half I am going to gamble. I know the risk. Yet I am going to win. I'm going to take my revenge, I am going to get my money back. I'll recover and get back on my feet again. Do you understand?

The agent had seen the visitor nodding, obviously frightened and yet awed by the force and determination he was witnessing in the other man.

"We'll attempt the impossible, no, we'll achieve the impossible, you and I. We'll challenge the system on a global scale. We shall have our revenge.

Diack had seemed to pause, to quieten himself. Then he had continued.

"You have finished your research on the golfers I asked? Good. The two of us will sit down now, go through your notes on them and work out our plan. Then we'll make our judgment and proclaim openly our verdict. An open verdict before a world audience."

Though the agent told me about that scene, he could make little of a guess as to what exactly it had been about. And of course from time to time the two men had got up, made themselves a drink and walked around. However the details about the dealings of *Diack*

Technologies that I had looked up online on my cellphone had given me enough to understand what Diack must have planned as a last resort. And at last I had discovered there what that 'fazer' word was, or whatever it had been that I overheard that Wednesday night in the marquee by the Dewhurst Stand at Perth Races.

And the only person he would have told this to was the man who had accompanied him to that house in the Bahamas.

"You know what my company's been doing over the last five years but you don't know everything. One thing I kept from you and has been highly secret is the aerospace engineering R&D our *Diack Technologies* have been doing with the US Department of Defense and Air Force Research Labs.

It took us time but we developed a portable unit named the MPHaSR, a mobile personnel halting and stimulation response laser. Fancy names they come up with huh? But its real. You can check it out online for yourself. It exists and is further ahead than most people are aware."

In fact I did look it up, the moment I became aware of how the acronym was spelled and what it stood for. And it really did exist.

Diack must have continued much as follows.

"In simple terms this gadget is a non-lethal kinda laser gun. It works by slightly dazzling the target in the eyes. Doesn't cause any lasting or damaging effect, just a couple of seconds of dazzling, like a sudden burst of sunlight on the eyes.

Our tech guys produced and tried out on tests a model

that's now miniaturized. In essence it looks now like a bulky digital 35mm SLR camera with a long lens. Must be mounted of course so we use a monopod. Range about 170 yards. Fully tried and tested. But to be sure, our tech guys who've trained on it for the past five months in the field will again try it out on selected golfers on the practice days of the British Open.

You and I are going to go over the field of this British Open for next year and select 60 top golfers who might just win the championship in St. Andrews in July. No certainty of course that we can hobble them all, but the chances of doing it for the top dozen or so are better than good.

We've got pretty good odds that we'll do it correctly. In fact the odds are damn good. I was always a gambler and this time I'm out to win with a vengeance.

With the dirt and stories of bribery we've got on some of the guys we could do a bit of persuading on them if we had to. After all, we're not going to ask them to lose the game or throw it all away. Just not win the damn tournament. We want McAvon, our man, to win the Claret Jug!

Only guy for sure we couldn't really affect is Jack Granger. He's a kingpin, won two British Opens one after the other so he's in there with a great chance. But I got a separate plan for him, one I'm damn sure is going to work. In that you'll play the major role. I'm counting on you.

Granger wears a highly reflective golf eyeshade. It's got an eight layer polarizing peak. And my laser just can't get past that. Never looks up when he strikes the ball. Just like all the good pros do, but his peak is also larger, curved and equipped with slight protective side shades, that are also polarized. So we just can't reach him. Can't do it. And by God we've tried and tried. So as I said, we got a special plan for him and for the Open. I'll tell you what we're going to do.

But first, to go back a bit, let's just think about money.

I've always gambled as you know. Gambled on leaving dear old Scotland, then England and going to Hong Kong with the company *Melville Erskine*. Gambled on leaving the company and starting my own in Hong Kong. Gambled on getting married. Gambled on marrying a Chinese wife and taking on loans to enlarge that company.

Gambled again on quitting Hong Kong and moving to the US. Gambled on going to the bankers there and taking on huge loans. These damn bankers, god crush their tiny souls. Got us into all this trouble in the first place, with their complacency and greed. Though they'll say the greed and the fault was mine.

But here's the plan.

We're going to make sure who wins the British Open. Yeah! Don't look at me like that. We're going to make the winner. And we're going to ensure that we have a bet on him. In fact we're going to ensure we have one hell of a bet on him. We're going to place five separate bets of $6000 or so each, one here in the Bahamas, two in Boston, a fourth in Hong Kong and the final one in London. Total then of $30,000 on the nose at near as dammit at odds of 500 to one or near as we can get. We'll do that just now in October, 10 months before the British Open in July on a rookie amateur. And we'll get a turnover of ten million plus. US.

And being so far in advance of the British Open, these greedy banker gamblers will grab our money and think us fools, to bank on an amateur and a rookie.

But that 10 million will push back my creditors, get rid of most of my debts and start me off a fresh, a new man. And you will get your slice too, and be off on that plane, Edinburgh-London Heathrow-Hong Kong, wherever.

But the odds on a simple gamble are not nearly good enough.

Even if the amateur Ritchie McAvon has in fact now earned himself a place in the British Open, by shooting a bogey-free 14 under par 62 and 66 at the 36 hole US Qualifier that gets him into the US Masters at Pebble Beach, and then into the important one, the British open Championship in St. Andrews. This is in fact the first time McAvon has made the cut in three attempts, for God's sake. Nearest he got was 11th in Texas a while back.

But McAvon is the man for me. And we'll make sure we enhance his prospects by hampering his most dangerous opponents in St Andrews, maybe even if we have to in the last resort by using the dirt we've found on them.

But much better with the MPHaSR.

And most of all by attacking Granger's peace of mind and self confidence.

Now how about all that? Sound too much of a long

shot? Maybe. But you know me. When I've started on something in the past, you know I've always worked at it till it succeeds. And you've nothing to lose, so far as a stake is concerned.

Give me your queries, your problems, your doubts. I'll sort them out, give you a slice of the action, the winnings, and pay your airfare Edinburgh-London Heathrow-Hong Kong. Let's sit down and work it out."

And so, the agent told me, he had watched as the two men had sat down, argued and discussed a lot, then eventually got up, shook hands.

And the man, Diack, had waved him in from the garden, to take the visitor back again to the airport.

"Did the visitor have a name?" I asked the agent.

"Sure, but fictitious as hell, I think," came the reply. "Way, or something."

CHAPTER THIRTY FOUR

"Granger well ahead in stakes to win third British Open Golf competition."

The headlines leapt out at me on my mobile as I sat at my balcony table in the Old Course Hotel. The red battery-low light also blinked at me and I promised to remind myself to charge the thing up real soon.

I skimmed the app and read another one.

A second news headline on the Open also pointed out that the betting odds on this year's golf championship winner had been steadily rising in favour of Jack Granger now for the past three months, so much so that most gambling authorities across the USA and Europe had now struck a very conservative and cautionary note where bets on Granger were now being placed.

Just where had that run on Granger started? I mused as I watched the crowds below throng up Links Road at the side of the 18th fairway. Well, to some extent it made good sense. Granger had been the clear winner of the Open the last time it had been played at Britain. He had won by three clear strokes in spite of a gusting southwest wind that had sprung up on the Thursday, the second day of play.

The pundits had declared Granger was one of the few overseas golfers, and about the only US one, to relish a battle on a course in blustery conditions. Of course the Pebble Beach youngster Ritchie McAvon was also mentioned in this respect. And the pundits pointed out that while Granger had experience on his side, McAvon had several years of relative youth in his favour.

In years past even Tiger, they pointed out, had won in Opens when the homeward conditions were relatively benign. Give any golfer on these Scottish links courses a wind in his face of 30 mph and gusting even higher at times and we would see what they were really made of. They would begin to lose heart and give in even well before the final back nine, those in the know maintained. Or were they just making news as dad sometimes pointed out?

I turned onscreen to the latest copy of the *Times* whose report on the coming Open I had already read and now read again, more carefully this time.

Any observer, such as the room lady, Angela, who asked if she could come in to clean as I read, might have thought that I was just indulging in reading about a favourite pastime. After all I had been around golf clubs all over now for the years and had even kept up a creditable handicap of nine for the past 5.

Yet there was more than just an amateur interest in my onscreen searches. My laptop and cellphone held over 50 reports related to the past five years of worldwide betting on golf results on a large scale throughout various countries and continents.

Nothing had yet been proved, but odd circumstances had hinted at a possible manipulation of results. It was certainly possible to the cynical, jaundiced or truly objective eye that the outcome of certain events had been odd and unexpected. Especially where the events relied on a single person-to-person competition, such as tennis or horseracing.

Or international golf.

I had to agree with some of these reports that such an event as the Open Golf Championship was a spectacle that raised passions and expectations on a huge scale in many areas of the world. Countries producing up-and-coming competitors from the likes of South Korea, Japan, China, South America and a host of other areas, were now achieving excellent golf scores and were more than capable of holding their own against the many accepted top-flight players from Britain, Ireland, South Africa, Australia and Scandinavia.

And the United States of America.

Could so many competitors from so many countries and backgrounds continue year after year to resist the blandishments and tempting sponsorship and cash offers thrown at them in a world that had become increasingly big business aware and where the pressure of expenses, travel and accommodation were a continual source of worry?

The reports here dealt with the frailties of human nature. In fact, with the greed of big businessmen who were aware of the clout they had, were proud of their ability to turn the world, its stock exchanges, government investments and research. And perhaps more recently been secretly attracted to the world of sport.

Yes, the ability to affect the outcome of a major sports championship such as the Open would be too much of an allure for some, I recognised. In my case, dad would have to be reminded and watch out.

I tapped in a reminder on my cellphone to speak to dad about it that night, the evening before the big final day and a time when nerves were at their most tense.

Yet for the life of me I just couldn't see how the outcome of such an event as this one could possibly be manipulated without it being blatantly obvious.

And surely the R&A had operatives around the course and elsewhere to counteract any such fiddle de dee.

08.30. The battery-low light was still blinking but I just had to get out and on course. Later. I'll charge the thing later. And economise on it in the meantime. Time I got out and on to the course. I knew Greg had already left and had secured yet another ride in the blimp.

CHAPTER THIRTY FIVE

You remember I stumbled on the steps at the R&A clubhouse Thursday morning? Well, on Saturday morning I had put a new elastic bandage on the thigh I scraped on Thursday. Not that I felt that I needed it but it was better to be safe than sorry.

It turned out it was just as well I did.

Anyway, 68 players had made the final cut and were here for the weekend. Dad and Ritchie McAvon among them. The big scoreboard now showed McAvon in the lead, 7 below par after 36 holes, and dad 5 below. Still the favourite, it seemed but flagging slightly. I wondered what was worrying him, if anything was. To me he seemed a little below his normal self and I could see George Orr trying hard to boost him up a bit on this important Saturday.

Diack was standing watching, smiling as always,

radiating confidence and bonhomie to all around.

I figured only the last 8 pairs out would be in contention, matches 27 to 34. And as it turned out, the punters and Alex Diack seemed to have agreed with me.

The weather had turned cloudy bright, a slight wind rising occasionally to 9-10 mph from the south-west now. A hint of higher winds and a change of direction for tomorrow, the final day,

CHAPTER THIRTY SIX

Peter Graichen, the window cleaner, told me later it was almost unbelievable.

As we had done before, Greg and I had gone to the practice ground with Granger and Orr. However a nagging doubt worried me and so I kissed Greg and muttered, "Off to the Blimp again? Look, enjoy. I'll catch you up later."

I moved round and paused first to speak to my friend the window cleaner again. There seemed to be more than just window cleaning in his job description. He saw too much, perhaps knew more than he should.

"What do you think of dad's chances now, Peter?"

Graichen smiled and glanced up at the clubhouse before replying.

"Better than most I think. Granger seems to get better with each passing day. He had a good three days practice and he now seems more relaxed than I seen them in a while. But you should know better than I."

I smiled back.

"True. I've not seen him look so good in a long while. I hope it continues. I look forward to seeing what today brings."

Peter said he'd been working on the general refurbishment and cleaning of the proposed new hotel, cleaning windows on the top floor room of the Hamilton Hall building, behind the 18th green.

He'd felt sure something was up, but not what.

Suddenly he had paused in his window cleaning and looked across to his right. He could hardly believe what he was seeing, looked away then looked again.

Poking out just slightly above the chimney pot of one of the houses half way down Links Road and suspended on what looked like a slim flat plastic rod was a pair of panties.

A pair of pink women's panties.

He shook his head after a moment and dismissed any thoughts he might have had about this strange apparition. Young people these days, he thought to himself. Anything goes.

Mind you, in a university town, even in the summer recess, they'll get up to anything and so its not that unusual, when you think about it. Still …!

AS I remember it, Greg also told me later about seeing these panties, and me, from the blimp as the cameras scanned the scene. But the reaction of the commentary crew and the technicians had been the same as Graichen's.

Student pranks.

More serious ideas had crowded into Graichen's mind.

He had realised that morning that there was now huge betting flooding in on the winner(s) of Open. And young McAvon had taken over the favourite's position.

He supposed Granger had blown it.

And it was then that Peter says he saw me, way below him near the R&A Clubhouse on his right. And it was then he decided to skip his job for a moment or two and come down and see me. Maybe to console me, maybe to boost my morale.

He caught up with me just as I was about to head off towards the second hole again.

"Amy! Amy!"

I turned back to find him waving at me.

I waited as he came up to me.

"How're things today? Leg ok?" he asked, looking me anxiously in the face.

I remember thinking he was looking a bit odd. I brightened up a bit for him, said things were fine and he seemed a bit relieved at that.

He took my arm and we strolled back towards the clubhouse. I had time anyway. Dad wasn't due out till later, and Greg, as I said, was up in his balloon. So what the heck.

We strolled a bit and chatted about this and that. Peter mentioned carefully that the betting seemed to have swung and was now largely in McAvon's favour. I said nothing much about that, except that things always swayed a bit to and from on the odds, especially on the last two days of an Open.

I made no mention of the texts and e-mails dad had received and the pressure he was under, quite apart from the stress of a wife who had left him and all the uncertainty of

a prestigious golf championship like this one.

It was then I noticed he was steering me away from the course and up towards Hamilton Hall.

"Got a minute?" he eventually asked me.

I nodded.

"I'm working on the windows of Hamilton," he continued. "Only got a couple of minutes off at the moment, but I think you should maybe come and go upstairs here for a bit. You get a great view from up here. And I've got something funny to show you. Made me laugh this morning. Let me show you what I mean."

And Peter took me up to his third floor vantage point, and nodded towards Links Road.

At first I couldn't see what he was on about. I looked all down the road, at the parked cars and the passers by. A man in a house in the Links Road, standing at a window with a pair of binoculars in his hands. The same scene as normal, I thought to myself.

Then I saw it.

High on a roof top of a house on Links Road. Flapping in the breeze. That pair of pink panties. Except what I didn't tell him was that I thought I recognised the floral pattern on them. I'd seen them more than once on the rotary drier at our Boston house.

Mother's pink panties.

"You can't really see them from ground level," Peter smiled.

We moved away and came downstairs again. Peter's attempt to cheer me up had had its affect. But the recognition of the panties had had a double effect on me. In one way it had cheered me to think I might now know where mom was and the fight and determination to escape that there might still be in her. That idea was fantastic.

And yet, how could I get to her? The house the panties were flying from was the same as the one where the man with the binoculars watching from the large ground floor windows.

I laughed, dutifully I felt at the time, but couldn't wait to get back down the stairs and on to Links Road, leaving Peter to carry on with his window cleaning inside and out.

Coming out of Hamilton House, I waved goodbye to Peter, as I moved uncertainly back in the direction of the R&A clubhouse.

Looking up now I noticed two things. One, Peter was quite right. From here on ground level there was no sign of the panties above. And two, the man with the binoculars in that house had them trained, I was sure, one me. Yet I couldn't really stare long enough in that direction to be sure.

I moved away, walking off along the path in front of the clubhouse shop and on past the green wooden fence bordering the 18th green. The crowds here were dense and growing denser by the hour as this second last day's play continued.

At the end of the fence where it met the narrow links road running down the side of the 18th fairway I stopped and looked back up at the top floor of Hamilton Hall.

Then I turned and glanced up quickly towards the Links Road. I could see that the man at the ground floor windows of the building still had his binoculars to his eyes.

Was it my imagination and was that man with the binoculars in fact watching me or just the 18th tee and the crowds around it?

Why would anyone be watching **me**? Unless of course they recognised me as Jack Granger's daughter. Yes, that would be it.

And were those panties flying from the chimneystack in fact mom's, or just something similar? There must be many pairs of red panties around, with a floral pattern. Not many flying from a chimney stack admittedly. But…

I watched the man at the window now more carefully, yet glancing at him only at odd moments and for a short time.

I saw him as he laid the binoculars down and I was almost sure I saw him frown.

He continued to watch me, I thought as I walked past the 18th green area and crossed the narrow links road towards the shops, hotels and guest houses that lined it.

That's what I was thinking, but now I supposed I was getting paranoid. First the panties. Now the idea I was being watched. And so what if people were watching me? I was after all the daughter of a famous golfer, one of the star attractions of this championship and this weekend.

Play it cool, girl I told myself.

I didn't dare look up now but I was sure he had watched me a little while longer then disappeared from the window.

I decided to walk down along the sidewalk, looking around me like some sightseer or tourist as I went. Abruptly and for no good reason that I could fathom, I raised my eyes to look at the upper floors of the other buildings around, Then I slid my gaze quickly round down the road. And as I did that, I caught a glimpse of the man now standing further back in that ground floor room with its big windows. Was that odd, or was it just me? He was half in shadow now.

What I had done and what I had seen, though I didn't know it, had decided my fate.

I'd memorised the position of the house and idled down along Links Road till I got level with the front door.

As I came level with the house and its half panelled front door, I noticed a figure behind the glass panel of the door.

I stepped forward without thinking and found myself within a foot or so of the door. I could see nothing unusual about it. But then why should there be? I saw there was no name plate on the door.

There was nothing unusual to be seen, three stone steps and a railing up to a solid oak door with glass panel and a heavy brass knocker below. No doorbell. Two large windows downstairs, with large heavy velvet curtains drawn to each side.

I stepped back a moment and looked up. Two more windows on the next floor, curtains drawn. A single window high above that, almost set into the apex of the roof. With an old stone lintel running along below, stretching from one side of the roof to the other.

No sign of panties. And yet…

I slung my shoulder bag more securely round my right arm, took a deep breath, stepped forward again and wondered just how foolish I was making myself.

Standing on the top step in front of the door I raised the brass knocker and let it fall heavily against the brass base plate. It seemed to make a loud noise to me. But nothing happened.

I thumped with the knocker twice. Louder this time.

For a second or two absolutely nothing happened. I've got it wrong, I thought. Massively wrong. Made a complete idiot of myself. Should never have paid any attention to that poor man at the window. Or the red panties I had seen from above.

A pair of eyes eventually appeared to my left, behind the curtains that a hand had drawn back just a bit behind the window.

I was completely taken aback, so much so I neither yelled nor resisted as far as I can remember. And no one seemed to have noticed a thing. But then it was St Andrews in the summer season. And The Open week.

Still nothing much happened. But bolder now and with nothing to lose I leaned forward and took the knocker in my hand for the third time.

At which point the heavy door was suddenly pulled open and a pair of hands grabbed me and pulled me inside.

The door closed abruptly behind me and I found myself in the arms of a thickset man, Chinese I thought, but I couldn't be sure and he was wearing some kind of a small face mask. It had all happened so fast.

The man held me tight. I couldn't move. He started to push me forcibly further into the house along the corridor.

The only thing I was aware of doing now was stumbling and falling on the wooden floor. As he dragged me along, I did the only thing I could. I fell. Or pretended to fall, ending up on top of the man as we collapsed to the floor. He fairly had a grip on me now though, and I could not get loose. The only thing I could do was scream, roll with him, and in doing so block his vision.

In the general flurry and confusion of arms and legs, I slipped my small cellphone from the outside flap of my bag, then pushed it frantically up under my skirt and into the top of the elasticated bandage round my thigh.

The man found his feet. His strength was enormous. He ripped my bag off my shoulder, pulled my jacket down over one arm then forced the other arm up in a lock against my back.

He forced me upstairs, and up another flight of stairs after that. For some reason I had not uttered a scream. Not a shout. I was totally shocked.

He pushed me again, pulled out a key and unlocked the door in front of him.

I was propelled forward, to end up lying gasping and panting on the hard wooden floor of a small, darkened room.

Where my mother stood before me.

CHAPTER THIRTY SEVEN

Imagine then Laura's delight and sorrow combined, when she heard the key in the lock at an unusual time, saw the door opening, the same man entering, but pushing before him a young woman. Me, Amy.

No attempt was made to prevent us from talking. He closed the door, then reappeared a few moments later with a tray he placed on the floor. He stood there and checked things over for a few seconds then left, locking the door, and I fell into mom's arms.

"Amy honey, I'm so glad to see you but how did you get here and what's that bandage on your leg?"

It was all mom could do to prevent herself from crying, while laughing at the same time.

In fact I was the one who began to and it was Laura wiped the tears from her daughter's face.

"The bandage's nothing mom. Really. Just a scrape

from a while back. And anyway, I used the bandage to stick my cellphone in before these goons could take my shoulder bag off me and search me. Look" and in triumph I showed her my cellphone. Which showed a dull red light. Battery now completely gone. Dead as a dodo. So much for my great attempt at subterfuge and keeping my cellphone so we could at least communicate. I suppose it was because I was walking too near this house, mom. I didn't really 'know what I was doing. With the window cleaner's help I'd talked my way into Hamilton Hall up there and got a great view from the top left window. Could see right down the 18th and onto the road just below here.

So then I came down, and just walked up and down the road outside, Links Road. I'd run out of ideas so I tried to look in the window downstairs."

I smiled at my stupidity.

"Must have looked too closely I suppose, and one guy, the guy who brought me upstairs, the Chinese guy with the sticky-out ears just rushed out and grabbed me, hustled me inside, roughed me up a bit then brought me up here. Never spoke a word, the two of them, just goons really.."

"And your leg, how did you do that?"

"Going up the clubhouse steps one day I slipped. Fell and scraped my thigh. Nothing to it, but a window cleaner and the medical lady in the R&A Clubhouse played overkill and saw to it that I was inspected, treated and cared for. You know how it is. If you've anything to do with Jack Granger the people around you go into overkill.

I stopped and held my hand up to my mouth, thinking what I had just said must have affected mom. What with the running away thing and all.

Then it struck me. Mom hadn't run away or deserted dad at all. She'd been kidnapped!

I grabbed mom and hugged her some more before I could go on.

"Anyway, after breakfast this morning I managed to slip as I was coming out the rear door of the Old Course hotel. The manageress persuaded me to see the resident medical staff and the lady there wrapped this double stretch bandage around my right leg. It has its advantages though. When the two goons grabbed me and bundled me inside, they searched me and took all my belongings but I slipped my cell phone down the inside of the bandage. It's still there but I don't know how good the battery is as I haven't managed to charge it up for three days now. But there might just be something in it."

Mom reached out and hugged me. "You being here has certainly raised my hopes. Before you came I hadn't the faintest idea where on earth I was. So where am I?"

"You're in St. Andrews, Scotland, in an old gable-roofed house on Links Road just by the 18th fairway. And by the look of it we are on the very top floor, probably the attic."

"Amy we can't do a thing about it. Can't even see much out. They've screwed a board across most of the window, there's just a small gap at the bottom but you can't see much through that slit and nobody can hear us or see us. There might be a maid or a housekeeper of some sort but I never see her and she never sees me or hears me. So we're stuck. By the way what day is it?"

"Saturday, Saturday evening." And I smiled at her. "Dad was just starting his third day when I got myself into this mess. I wonder if he and Greg will notice I'm missing." Mom sat down on the bed. "Probably neither of them will until dinner or after. So dad made the cut for the weekend?"

"You bet he did! He's done well, considering. But when I last saw him, he still had that kinda hang dog look about him. Little wonder, I suppose, considering what he's been through. Nearest guy with him is Ritchie McAvon, two strokes ahead. He slowly but surely has made his way up the scoreboard and if McAvon doesn't win it, which looks more than likely, then I would bet on dad."

I looked round the room. "Not much stuff in here is there, mom?"

"No, there's not. I've been looking around it for what, five, six days now and I just can't figure any way to make it out of here." Mom shrugged. "Only thing that lets in air here is that dammed fireplace over there." She nodded towards the small fire and its surround.

"When I'm trying to sleep I can hear the wind blowing over the chimney pot up there." Mom pointed up towards the roof. "If you look up the chimney you can see the sky above, but the hole's so small you couldn't get up it."

I got up from the bed, walked across to the fireplace,

went down on my hip and one elbow, then came back and sat on the bed beside mom.

"See what you mean, mom. Couldn't even get my head up that chimney, no way."

Then I got up and walked across to the window.

The room, if the tiny enclosed space way up in the pointed roof of the house could be called that, seemed to be lit by a small, narrow window, almost entirely boarded up and set right up in the v-shaped apex of the building.

CHAPTER THIRTY EIGHT

Smooth talking Greg had persuaded the engineers in the Blimp to allow him to sift through hours of recorded tv video. They believed he was just fascinated by the footage taken but in fact my Greg was searching for any scene that might be relevant to any unusual or odd events that might have happened on the course or near it.

Particulaly views of the 9th hole area, the lovely River Eden water and of course Leuchars airfield in the background.

And lo and behold, as Greg texted me, he did find one odd little view. A brief background shot of the green on the 9th hole, with the river and of course the airfield behind. And there way in the distance the shot showed a plane coming in to land, last Sunday morning.

A Learjet, as he had been able to make out eventually.

A car had appeared and stopped by the control tower. Two men from the tower came and waited beside the car.

The jet had landed from the west, taxied off the runway and up towards the control tower where it had stopped and chocks had been slipped in.

After a while the door had swung open, two men had appeared at the top of the steps and the two other men from the tower had climbed up and entered. One in civvilian clothes, the other in RAF uniform.

Yet another shot twenty minutes or so later had shown, though still at that distance, the two men leaving and going back to the tower.

Fifteen minutes later a folded wheelchair had been lowered down the steps, a person had been carried down by one of the two men from the Learjet, the person placed in the wheelchair and pushed off towards the waiting car. That was all.

The camera practising on that 9th hole area had then swung round to practise framing views of the southern approaches to the area, as well as shots to the dunes, sands and sea on the east.

CHAPTER THIRTY NINE

It was Saturday evening when Granger got the final e-mail.

I had made all the arrangements for him, as you know. How to use the cellphone. Not to use it on course, where cellphones were banned to players. To use texting or e-mail instead of actual verbal mail as often as possible. Charge it up every night. Huh! Some teacher me! Hadn't even kept my own phone charged.

Talking to fathers about cellphones is sometimes like talking to a child.

I had also insisted he kept it with him whenever and wherever he could, as I told you, though I knew for a fact he sometimes forgot and sometimes just plain didn't take it with him. And some of the time he didn't want to have it near him.

I remember thinking also that it might raise dad out of

the depression after his Laura's disappearance.

There had been word in the media before about a possible breakdown in their marriage, hints that Granger had been seen with another woman while on tour. Even other women. Plural. Granger and Laura however had always denied any rumors of a rift.

Anyway dad kept it mostly by him and checked it from time to time now each day. But sometimes of course e-mails came to him and announced themselves, discretely but insistently. As one did that Saturday evening.

The man in the mask, the man with the ears, had come back into our attic room later that evening, about 6 or so, but I couldn't be sure. How I missed my watch! He held a handgun that he put down on the floor beside him. How evil that looked, that gun.

He took mom and tied her again to the wooden chair, as dad and I had seen in the other video e-mail dad had been sent. Those sticky-out ears of his mesmerised me.

I was made to sit down crossed-legged in front of her. I wasn't tied but the man spoke now at last, making it perfectly obvious what we were each to do. He definitely sounded foreign. An American accent to his English, and yet a few odd words here and there. Asian, I remember thinking at the time.

We were not to say a word, just look into his cellphone's lens. To make no movements or signs. In short, to give whoever the viewer was to be, and I was sure now it was to be dad, no clue as to where we were or what was happening.

We were not to give a clue, but my brain was running overtime. If this video were to be
e-mailed like the other one, then it would have to be sent either tonight or early tomorrow, Sunday morning.

No doubt the sight again of his wife and now his daughter too was intended to give Granger the final threat, the final push to force him to throw the Open tomorrow. Or at least to play with little conviction and desire to win.

So dad was to lose, and McAvon was to win. Simple. But nasty.

It didn't take long. The guy shot the short video, then moved me well back and released mom. He left and our room fell silent again for a while. Neither mom nor I could think of anything to say except to hug each other and commiserate each other that the final screw was to be applied to dad. He would get the video soon and there was no way of him avoiding second place at best now.

About twenty minutes after, dad told me later, Granger's cellphone chimed, loudly so he couldn't fail to notice an e-mail or text had come in.

He was with Greg in his hotel room when this happened. Greg watched as dad opened his phone and flicked the blinking e-mail icon.

This time there was no preamble. No introductory text. Just a plain attached e-mail with a simple title. *Family Shot.*

Of course dad had eventually panicked when there was no sign of me nearby as he and George Orr had gone round the course that Saturday. Dad had played ok but it was clear to George that things were not right, that dad was having difficulty keeping his concentration. But dad had stuck at it, George told me.

By the end of the round, when dad and he were finally alone, after a couple of tv interviews and one for the Washington Post and the Boston Herald, George told me dad had shown his true feelings.

"If Amy's gone and left us now, as well as Laura, then I've had it, George," dad had said.

And as time had gone on and I hadn't appeared, even though Greg had, things began to get bleaker and bleaker for dad.

This e-mail he now got was the last straw, and the fact that it showed the two of us, his wife and his daughter, captured and held together in that awful room, wherever it was, was almost too much for him.

It had taken all Greg's persuasion, cajoling and determination to calm dad down and eventually to get him out of that hotel room, lovely though it was but now with too many memories over the past week.

The two of them had gone downstairs, into the Jigger Inn, to get away, as I said, from the room above and even the hotel lobby area.

They had sat there the two of them, dad not saying much, Greg doing most of the talking. I would have figured that. Greg was always a talker.

They had chosen a table outdoors and one facing away from the course, towards the west as it happened and looking out towards the road.

And it was some time later, when neither of them was

really sure after, that it happened.

CHAPTER FORTY

They sat there the two of them apparently, saying little or nothing now and staring into space.

Greg, from what I know of him, had probably just about given up by now. And the two of them must have been thinking what Sunday, the final day of the Open, would bring. Despair might have been too good a word for it, no doubt.

It was dad who saw it first.

He was looking at a row of vehicles parked a little to the side of the Old Course Hotel's car park, out beyond the little building with its lovely clock.

And dad found himself staring, without thinking really about it at all, at one particular vehicle. A large 4x4, parked right on the end of the line in the evening light.

And then staring absent mindedly at a man who had suddenly appeared, tipped off the hotel doorman who had brought out his bags and put them in the rear of the four wheel drive, then climbed into the nearside driver's seat.

It suddenly hit him. The man was Alex Diack. Dad tapped Greg on the shoulder and pointed in the direction of the car

Now that was strange, dad thought. Looked like Diack was taking his leave, what with his luggage and all having been loaded into the offroader.

In fact, Diack had now reversed the car out of the parking slot, swung the front wheels round and was even now heading out the car park exit.

Why, dad thought, and Greg had had exactly the same idea, why was such a professed lover of golf, someone who had spent a fortune getting here, with his Learjet and presumably also his Cadillac Escalade being ferried across the Atlantic for his convenience and pleasure, why would such a person of wealth and influence leave now, on the eve of the final round of the 150th Open?

It made no sense.

Of course, businessmen occasionally had to make sudden and important decisions. Like leaving a place suddenly if the demands of their profession compelled them. And perhaps Diack now simply had to get up and go.

Still, it was unusual.

"Roomy car that," dad said.

Greg was just about to nod in agreement, thinking of how it had ferried them all to the races and back in comfort and style, when the word 'roomy' struck him.

That was exactly the car he had found in the back video

shots from the Blimp. The vehicle the guys had videoed coming up last Sunday to the Learjet at Leuchars.

And from that jet had come two people, and one other person. Who had been carried down the aircraft steps by a burly, strong man. And placed into the Cadillac.

A roomy dark blue Cadillac Escalade. Diack's Cadillac. Greg was excited now. He half turned and put his hand on Granger's shoulder. What else was it he had to remember now? What small fact had he forgotten, ignored? Something that surely was vital to his understanding of things?

It came to him.

'Roomy'. Of course!

Not just the Cadillac had been roomy. So had the Learjet! And one part of the jet now came to mind. The roomy lounge. And the long, locker-type bench seat there.

Of course the jet would have been thoroughly searched by the customs guys when it had landed at Leuchars. And that removable bench seat lid too would have been take off and checked. As no doubt the crew and passenger had been too.

So no way to smuggle a thing, or a person, into UK, it would appear. But if you looked at things slightly differently, then another possibility existed!

Greg put both hands on dad's shoulders now and turned dad to face him.

How sad and dejected Granger's face looked now. Yet maybe there was news.

"Dad," and that apparently was the first time Greg had

called him 'dad', "dad who would have thought of smuggling something OUT of the USA?"

Dad stared at Greg in non comprehension.

"Greg, what do you mean? What are you talking about? Diack has just left to head out towards Edinburgh airport presumably. Flying out of UK. And his Cadillac will no doubt be air freighted out soon after he leaves."

"Yes," Greg nodded and dad noticed he actually smiled. "But the person the Blimp cameras recorded Sunday past as coming out of Diack's Learjet at Leuchars could have been kidnapped and smuggled OUT of Boston Logan. Drugged and hidden beforehand, say in the hangar, in the empty space, the roomy locker space in the Learjet's lounge bench seat."

"And then brought out during the flight, " dad caught on, "drugged again near landing time at Leuchars, and brought out, with a passport, fake or otherwise, then driven away with her wheelchair."

Greg nodded.

"Driven away and hidden away in that room we saw in the video." And Greg really smiled now. "The same room where Amy is now too."

And all the two of them had to do was find us.

CHAPTER FORTY ONE

Laura drew me over to the fireplace, placing a warning finger over her lips to keep me from making a noise as the two of us knelt and listened to the voices in a room below.

Two people were talking, two men, and obviously close friends, but who they were was not clear. Presumably the man who had pulled me into the house and another.

I almost recognised the voice of one of them, but the flue seemed to echo and distort his words.

The more forceful of the two was talking now.

"We drew up a list of the world's top 25 golfers we expected to take part in the Open at St Andrews and make the final cut for the last two days of the golf.

I know well the chances this entailed, that one or other might be injured before the event took place, or fall ill, or just play impossibly badly on the day, or whatever.

I was taking chances. But it was better than taking my financial losses and doing nothing to recover. Not to say that I had also set about trying to re-structure my company, rethinking its strategies and reluctantly cutting back on its resources.

I can tell you, I wept. I punched the wall and wept at my losses. Money I'd spent so long building up and safeguarding. But I refused to keep on weeping, ringing my hands and going under.

"If nothing else I'm a fighter. And I'll always take a chance rather than let others tell me what's going to happen.

And I've trusted no one. No one that is, apart from the one friend and true believer in me, you.

"Anyway, we spent days, months, researching on the internet and elsewhere, checking and re-checking on these top 25 golf athletes.

I sent you out, to speak to people, to universities, and golf clubs, friends, neighbours and acquaintances of these golfers. We sat down, talked over the info you had collected. And we whittled the list down to 7."

At this point one of the men must have moved a way from the fireside below, for the conversation became muted and inaudible now. I feared we'd heard the last of the talk and I was just about to speak when mum shushed me again with her finger.

"… seven men good and true. Or not so good, in some cases. Mistakes of youth, wrong judgements, sexual flings, embarrassments, financial errors, drugs, anything that had been a hidden blemish on these golfers' characters. That was what we looked for. And found. And might be forced to use. Though I definitely don't want to. All in all we don't want to force these guys to throw the game away. We don't want them to lose anything. Just not to win the damn championship! But we've also got the cameras. And our four operators of these will not leave with the others but stay to the very end, just in case they're needed."

I heard a clink of glasses and something being put down on a glass table. A wind also seemed to be getting up, for I could hear it whistling in the chimney. But mum held my arm as the words from below came again.

"The top man's undoubtedly Jack Granger. Granger has now won five Grand Slams, as I think of them. Five majors in golf. And two of these have already been UK Opens.

So this man has the ability, the determination and an outstanding track record over the past ten years. He's the one most likely to refuse to cooperate. Can't be bribed or cajoled. But the higher they rise, the more vulnerable they become."

Laura and I heard a laugh and then a clink of glasses.

"But Granger's got a vulnerable wife!

Not that Laura Granger's a liability. Far from it. She obviously adores her husband, has supported him through thick and thin until he had made good, first in the USA, then abroad, and now most of all that Jack Granger's at his pinnacle. But now we have the second ace in the pack, his beautiful 18 year old daughter."

More laughter. Mom held my arm and squeezed tight,

staring into my face.

"The fact that each evening in Boston where they lived, Laura was in the regular habit of going out jogging, that was a bonus for us. And the solution.

She is, she was an inveterate jogger. And therefore vulnerable. And we have her, and the daughter."

Again there was a pause and I feared the two had moved away from the fireplace side for good. But in time the voices returned.

"The remaining six golfers are good. In fact the top 25 or so are damn good. Each good enough to win the Open here in St Andrews.

And yet with the character flaws you unearthed, flaws that I believed I could use to manipulate them or put them off, we can control them. If need be. Or use the camera guns if we absolutely have to. One short millisecond flash in their eyes at the appropriate moment is all we need. But only if we have to.

And I could remind each or any of these men of their flaw, if the time comes.

For some it's a peccadillo with another golfer's wife. For others it's a small, forgotten criminal record from way back. Or a hidden asset that the inland revenue people would love to know of. It goes on and on. Flaws, weaknesses, a vulnerability. There's one in each and every one of us, the more's the pity.

And in Granger most of all. I've acted on him and with these two little doves locked in upstairs we've got him where we want him."

There was a pause in the conversation again. As if the

two men were reflecting, thinking over the day ahead. Then the talk resumed.

"But the one that's different, the main man, is the outsider. Ritchie McAvon.

On this man, this fantastic young newcomer from Pebble Beach, we placed last October our wagers to win at the huge rookie odds of 250-1 and in a couple of cases even more. Fifty thousand lovely US greenback dollars. And a side bet to finish in the top 5 at 90-1. The stake money, carefully, selectively placed. Ten percent of the winnings of these two bets to go to you, my friend. And not a word about it mentioned. Ever."

Again there came a silence, and I wondered at the daring and the evil of the man below. Or was it evil, or just the sheer desperation of a man who'd almost lost all?

There was more.

"At times in my bed I've lain long awake, unable to sleep, my money, my future, my fortunes resting on this one piece of careful planning. On this outsider of a chance, that the one man I've selected, this rookie from Pebble should now prove man enough to win a most prestigious golf championship. In the face of seasoned golfers from all over the world. With the whole world watching. Over four different and differing days. Thursday to Sunday. And now he's almost there. And we have it all worked out. At of all venues the home of golf. St Andrews.

Madness? Genius? Pure dead reckoning? The end of *Diack Technologies* Inc?

The end of me? Or something bigger than I've ever achieved before? If only my wife were alive to see it!

Over the last three nights in the hotel I've reviewed it all in his mind. I think we've got it made."

And there was another, and as it turned out, a final clink of glasses and the end of conversation that had so blown my mind, as I turned to mom and hugged her in a desperate and close embrace.

All of us now, the two downstairs and us two above in our locked and darkened room, consigned ourselves to our fate.

And to the events of the coming day.

The men below seemed to be gambling all or nothing. If they were not to use the dirt they gathered about the Various top golfers then how could they be so sure their man McAvon would win? And what were these camera things they had talked of?

CHAPTER FORTY TWO

It must have been about 6pm that Saturday. Mom was dozing on the bed in our prison room and I was sitting on a stool by the fireplace, listlessly thinking about the website of *Diack Technologies* and the ups and downs of the company and its CEO, Alex Diack. But the battery on my cellphone was now of course dead and I could access nothing, let alone make a call or text. Some bright spark me.

All at once I heard again voices from below coming up the chimney flue. But I felt sure there were two people there, one doing virtually all the talking.

The first voice I heard I couldn't identify. But the words this man spoke were clear and obviously with the feeling of someone who knew the listener well. But who was it? And who was the other?

"You were a different man from the one I had known for years," the voice said. "You had lost your wife suddenly, early. You'd made a fortune but no longer had a wife or family. No one to enjoy your wealth with, no one to give it to.

You were a man who'd then been stripped of much of your fortune when the economic devastation had come upon the world. Your company had been decimated. Your personal and business life had been greatly impoverished, but you kept up appearances and planned and fought to regain your former status. I admire for all that, as I've always admired you.

A man whose only real friend is the person speaking now."

There was a pause and even from a distance away from the speaker and a voice distorted at times by the resonance of the flue I could sense the tension and the feeling between the two persons below. Was the other a man? I couldn't tell, for the second person as yet had not spoken a word.

The voice, the man spoke again.

"I've directed this whole thing for you from the start, keeping you at arms length from it, so that nothing can come back to you. And I've kept myself in the background hidden from the two upstairs, as we agreed."

There was a murmuring from downstairs, but nothing clear, nothing vital I could seize on use to identify the speaker, let alone the listener.

"We'll now set up the final scenario to rebuild your company, your hard won empire. To recover part of the lost fortune, of the company and my share."

The voice came up the chimney flue to me fainter but

clearer now, as if the speaker had perhaps moved away a little.

"We've left the use of the PhaSR's till the very end. And I'm glad we made the decision to leave out any use of blackmail, other than with Granger. We had no option there, but we've managed it."

What on earth was a PHaSR? I wondered. But then the first speaker made it clearer for me, as I heard him resume.

"It was in some ways it was a minor miracle that our company found details of the PHaSR three years back online and took up development of it ourselves with the US Department of Defense. Still seems crazy to me that the details are still there for all to see online, but essentially its non lethal.

Miraculous we've made it to be portable, handheld, and much like a long lens camera on a monopod. Its laser flash affects the human target's eyes, in our case, golfers, but it's no more annoying or harmful than a flash of sunlight off a window, as we've proved. And much briefer – $1/3000^{th}$ of a second.

So, to sum up, we have McAvon set to win, Granger under our control, and all we need now are our PHaSR operators, four of them, to cover the last six pairs out tomorrow, Sunday. And they may or may not be needed. McAvon is to win, at the odds we placed on him. And we don't give a damn who else finishes where so long as no one beats McAvon.

With a bit of luck we won't have to use the PHaSR at all. The winner of an Open or a Masters nearly always comes from the last two groups out, never mind the last six.

So when the rest of us have made our escape I've seen to it the PHaSR camera guys will stay to the end. I've organised the choppers for them and the four of them all have their getaway air tickets and the long cruise bookings."

And then I heard the other, unnamed man ask.

"And yourself?"

These two brief words were the only ones I heard the second man ask. They were not enough or distinct enough for me to id him. And yet ...

"I got it. Chopper first from here. Then Edinburgh and from there online KLM to China, and once there I'll disappear for three years or so. Set up my own company with my wife and some of her relatives. We'll see. But I'm all set and I've seen to the boys on the course tomorrow. Don't worry. You take off tonight. You'll be over the hill and out of sight with no worries and our money restored."

There was a short pause, then I heard the second man speak again.

"And the two women?"

Again there was a pause, then came the reply from the first man.

"Don't worry about them. I've got a delayed text message that'll be sent to Granger and to his daughter's partner Greg, telling where they are. They'll be set free Monday."

And so the conversation ended, with me none the wiser

as to the two speakers, and only six words from the second speaker to go on. And yet that second speaker seemed to be in control, to be the boss.

I listened some more but there was nothing else. And after ten minutes or so I gave up and was left to simply wonder.

CHAPTER FORTY THREE

The window itself seemed to consist of two small rectangular panes and was an old sash window with a brass plate that had been screwed down into place across the two sliding sections of the window.

Without a screwdriver and possibly a chisel there was no way to force the window halves apart and slide either the top pane all the way down, or the bottom one up.

There was a period of silence as the two of us thought. Then I spoke again.

"Do they feed you again in this place?"

Mom shook her head. "Nope. That's it till lunchtime or even later tomorrow. What time is it anyway?"

I looked at mom.

"Haven't got the slightest, mom. They took my watch and everything else I had on me, 'cept for my cellphone and that's a goner for the time being. But by the sky up there it's getting darker now. Should be about quarter to

10 or so, I think. No light in here I suppose?"

"None at all, honey. We'll just have to make the most of it on this bed, the two of us. And we've only got this as one big long pillow here."

The two of us lay down and pulled the duvet over us.

CHAPTER FORTY FOUR

We had lain there like that for ten minutes or so. More restless than mom, I had wriggled and thrashed about trying to make myself comfortable when suddenly an idea hit me and I sat up and got out of bed.

"Mom, mom, did anyone take the tray away?

"No. The tray's still there and we haven't yet eaten much of the food anyway. Are you hungry? Remember, most of that food's got to last us till they bring more tomorrow."

Mom had sat up now too.

"Mom, I've got an idea. There are two knives still on that tray, aren't there?"

Laura nodded. "Yes."

I said nothing but began to feel my way in the semi gloom towards where the tray still must be lying on the floor.

There was still just enough light to see the knives on a plate beside two spoons and two forks. The knives were good solid silver plate, heavy handled and sturdy. I must confess my hopes had begun to rise.

I picked up one of the knives and made my way across to the wooden board over the window. A sliver of amber light from the street lamp outside shone through the slit between the bottom of the board and the bottom of the window sill.

With my fingers I guided the blade of the knife into the slot on one of the screws at the bottom of the board. I was real careful, trying not to let the blade of the knife slip, for it was just too slim to fit well into the groove of the screw nail. I began to twist the knife anti-clockwise. Yet despite my best efforts the screw didn't give at all, and finally the blade slipped sideways, bruising the thumb and forefinger of my left hand where I had tried to hold the screw and its plate firm.

"Damn!" I sucked my fingers and shook my head in frustration.

Realising what I was trying to do, mom had come across and was kneeling on the floor beside me.

Mom looked on in surprise and seemed about to speak, when she shut her mouth, thought a little and watched. If this works, I thought she was thinking, my daughter will just have shown some of the enterprise and original thoughts her dad has proved capable of over the years, whether he's on a golf course or not.

Sometimes he gets it all wrong. But then again he can try things which at first glance seem unusual and wrong, and often they turn out good.

Now I seized the knife with two hands and applied all the pressure I could, anti-clockwise.

Mom could see the immense effort I was applying, both to get maximum pressure on the screw and yet not overdo it or burst or twist the screw head or the knife blade. Four more times I tried with all my strength to try and twist the screw with the knife blade. I had not moved a fraction at all. I flung the knife down on the floor in disgust and fury.

Mom took over.

"Let me have a go. With all the rock climbing I've done in the States my fingers are maybe a mite stronger than yours." She picked up the knife and slotted the blade into the groove of the screw, as I had done.

I sat and sucked her bruised thumb.

Although she seemed to be applying more pressure on the screw than I had done, mom had no more success in turning the screw that I had, and after three or four minutes panting and grunting from mom the screw still stayed firmly in place.

"And this is just the first of four screws in this lower half of the two boards across the window," mom groaned. "We'll never get them loose!"

"Never mind, mom. We've got all night, and probably most of Sunday morning too, before the goons come back," I smiled. "Here, let me have a go again." And I took the knife from mom and tried again.

Several more minutes went by, I remember, with the two of taking turns to twist and turn and pant and groan in our efforts to move just one screw nail.

Without success.

The two of us sat there, our backs against the wall, thinking about how near and yet just how far we had come to finding this way out.

I think it was I who spoke next.

"Anyway, even if we get the screws out, and force the window open, how far are we above the ground? 20, 25 feet above the road below. We're high up, I think, almost at the apex of the roof here."

Mom nodded. "Just about as high as the chimney pots, I would guess."

She fell silent for a moment.

"Not that the height would bother me or you. We've been used to being higher up a cliff face in Montana than this, honey. That would be no sweat, for you or me."

I turned to gaze at my mother.

"Mom, is there coffee in that thermos on the tray?"

She turned and looked at me.

"Sure is. You're not thirsty are you? But then, I suppose with all that effort you've…"

"No, mom. It's not that."

I got up and crawled across to the tray on the floor. I picked up the thermos in one hand, in the other I took the only teaspoon I could find and crawled back on elbows and knees to the window.

I can remember mom looking on in frank amusement, with a puzzled frown.

I screwed off the thermos lid, then holding the thermos in my left hand, I carefully tried to pour some coffee into the small teaspoon I was holding in my right.

The coffee came out across the lip of the thermos in a rush, despite my best effort to take it slowly and control the flow. The floor below the window was soaked.

"Wonderful!" mom murmured. "Now we have that much less coffee for tomorrow."

I could find no sensible reply to that. Mothers always know how to make you look young and foolish again, don't they?

But holding the teaspoon level and keeping as much of the coffee in it as I could, I moved the spoon towards the screw we had both wrestled with and tipped the liquid, or as much of it as I could, on to the head and sunken stalk of the screw.

Mom watched and then understood.

"You're trying to get some liquid down into the screw hole to slacken it off a bit!" I nodded my head frantically in mock appreciation.

"You are a resourceful little soul, aren't you, daughter mine!"

"Not so much of the 'little' Mom, please."

"True, true, you're not little any more, are you honey. Cool! Give me five!" and she held up the palm of her right hand.

"Easy, mom! Easy. No need to try and be ultra cool, at your age."

She sighed.

"Mothers just can't win these days can they?"

"But they're still mothers. Just be yourself mom. I love you the way you are. Specially since I know now you didn't walk out on dad. Never did figure you for being like that anyway."

Mom cocked her head to one side, in thought then spoke. "Why don't we just pour some more coffee into the other screws now. All of them, top and bottom panel."

It was my turn to listen and then understand.

"Good thinking, mom. If we do it now, they'll maybe all have time to soak and slacken off, if they're ever going to, that is." And I held up one hand and instantly got a high five from mother. "Way to go, mom!"

I watched mom smile to herself. "So it's 'we' now, is it, 'if we do it now'. And smiled again.

There was a slight creak, and then the screw turned. Just a fraction or so, but it had turned.

"No high fives just yet, Amy, but carry on there honey. You're doing fine!"

I grinned, spat on the palms of my hands, and carried on. With the semi darkness in the room and the inefficiency of the knife as a screwdriver, it took a while before the two of us taking turns got that first screw out.

Then mom took up the other knife and set to work to undo the next of the four screws in the wooden upper panel boarding up the window.

I chipped in from time to time.

After many curses, much spitting on palms, and the total bending of the blade of one of the knives, we succeeded in getting all eight screws out.

Then, as quietly as possible in case anybody below might hear, we removed the two boards from off the small window and pushed to one side the sliding snib lock that held the window from opening.

A brief glance out, looking all round, showed a small stone balcony with windows below us, and above and to each side the v-shaped stepping stones of a gabled edge to the roof above.

"Good thing is," mom whispered, "the three windows below have a solid stone lintel beam above them."

I remember mom's stupid grin in the half light.

"And it's only about an arm's breadth to the crenellated gable blocks to our right. It's high and it's dangerous honey, but early tomorrow morning, or is it now this morning while the world hopefully is still asleep, we're going to do it. We're going to escape!" And she leaned over and kissed me.

Somehow she almost seemed to have taken over. But then, that's mothers for you.

By the time the two of us had soaked the eight screws, ourselves and the floor below, we reckoned we needed whatever was left of the coffee before proceeding, and sat to one side of the window sipping thoughtfully.

All at once I think I looked up at mom and asked.

"Is it still ok to have a prayer now and then, you know, a personal, heartfelt, desperate ask for real help?"

I watched as mom smiled again.

"Sure is, daughter mine, sure is. But we really have to need it, and mean it. I'll say no more."

There's that 'daughter' word again, I thought to myself, but said nothing. But there's that 'we' again too. Nothing like adversity for teaching you things.

CHAPTER FORTY FIVE

A fine rain shrouded the Open course, the clubhouse and the Old Course Hotel on the Links as Alex Diack backed his dark blue Cadillac Escalade out of the far side of the hotel car park and exit. He had reconfirmed by phone that his Cadillac Escalade would be collected from the Hilton carpark by Air Enhance and prepared for rapid airfreight to the USA the following morning.

He was off, leaving no lead to connect him either with the kidnapping of Lauren and Amy Granger or with the betting on the outcome of the St Andrews Open Golf Championship.

He turned onto links Crescent to join the A 91. Leaving St. Andrews by the small roundabout near the public car park, he headed out towards the M 92.

40 minutes later his wheels drummed a soothing rhythm as he took the outside lane across the forth Road Bridge.

At the south exit he followed the centre lane curving away out right to begin his approach towards Edinburgh and the dual carriageway leading towards the airport and his private jet at Turnhouse airfield.

The rain was still falling and the darkness had now settled in as he pulled off at the final around round into the Hilton forecourt. There he parked the Cadillac in the rear and at reception confirmed his overnight booking and that Air Enhance would collect the Cadillac in fifty minutes time.

After a quick supper in the restaurant and a last Glenlivet nightcap he settled in for the night and fell peacefully, contentedly asleep around ten.

His last thought was that he had planned it all well, set up the winner to perfection and that tomorrow as he flew home to Boston the results of the Open would confirm his achievement.

CHAPTER FORTY SIX

Neither of us knew whether the other had slept at all that night, and I'd told mom nothing about Lisa Brand's e-mail to my now dead cellphone, but I felt mom's hand on my shoulder, shaking me gently. Mothers do take over sometimes, if you let them.

"No idea what time it is, and it's only half light and the beginnings of dawn outside, she said.

"No one outside seems to be up and about. So I reckon we have the remains of the coffee and some of that rye bread and marmalade they've given us, and then we go. Ok honey?"

"Ok mom. It's a go." I can remember pausing, then trying it. "Mom," I looked at her, "Mom, can we discuss the affair of your panties that I saw fluttering above the chimney top outside here. The ones I saw from the top floor of Hamilton Hall. You know, the pink ones."

Mother rounded on me, her face a stone cold mask.

"I don't want to go there. Got it? It didn't happen."

I nodded.

The two of us then ate and drank in silence, listening for any sounds from below, but there were none.

Ten minutes later we stood by the half open window and made our plans from what we could see.

Mom definitely took over now, as the more experienced climber. But I kept the panties in reserve, at the back of my mind.

"I go first. No, no arguments. I can do it, and I'm going to do it. I'm going to wriggle out backwards and swing my legs down till I can touch the lintel below with my toes. Then I'll reach out and up and get my first hand grip on the side of the window and swing out to get a grip with my right hand across towards the gables."

Mom turned and hugged me.

"Look out for your bandaged thigh. I know its not bad now, but remember, all we have on our feet are sneakers. Not the best of footwear for this kinda climbing, but it'll have to do. As you saw last night, it's a short distance horizontally across to the gable blocks, but a hell of a way down if we blow it."

She kissed me, then worked her way backwards out of the window.

One helluva woman.

I had little doubt that mom would make it across to the gable. I was now not so sure of myself. The drop was considerable, on to hard unyielding tarmac or solid concrete. Only good thing was, I thought wryly to myself, the stone round the window was dry, and cool, though a wind had risen.

I stood back until mom had got fully outside the window and begun to move off to her right. Then I leaned out and watched.

I wished I hadn't. I wished I'd gone first, but too late for wishing now.

At first, mom's left foot slipped slightly on the tiny ledge that the lintel below provided. However, But she recovered, pressing in even closer to the stone face of the house and not once looking down to the roadway and iron railings below.

As I continued to shiver and watch, mom reached out further and further to the right, till her right hand got the best grip she could on the gap between the stone wall blocks.

I could see the blood drain from mom's finger tips as she pressed and gripped on what crevices she could find. At the same time, she inched her feet sideways, along the more solid projection of the lintel below.

Mom then seemed to pause. She was now only six inches or so short of reaching the far vertical edge of one of the gable blocks.

Lord, I'm praying again, I whispered, strangely thinking of the widow Lisa Brand on the Edinburgh Castle ramparts. Please listen to me, hear me. I'm praying for my mom to make it here, on the face of this gabled house on Links Road.

I held my breath and watched.

I saw mom take a deep breath and release one hand, her

right, then reach out to grip the stone gable block. The decisive moment, I realised. To do so, mom had to let go of the one sure hold that she had, and then move her feet sideways below.

She got it.

I saw mom move both feet into position below, then release her left hand and lean over quickly to seize the gable with both hands and arms. Having done that, she swung her legs and torso up and over to straddle the blocks of the gable.

She was there.

Mom lay there for what seemed an age to me before she at last swung her head round and gave me a weak smile. Sometimes mothers can fake it, but do it.

"Nothing to it, honey," she whispered. That was for me. She knew what I was going through.

"Like hell, I muttered to myself.

And now it was my turn.

Getting up and out through the small sash window was, if anything, the easy part, I realised. She dropped my feet down, down, till I reached the lintel edge below. I kept telling myself not to look down.

Remember all mom told me about cliff climbing, I told myself. And anyway, I tried to console myself, you just had a lesson, a reminder in rock climbing. You watched how mom did it. If she can do it, then I'm sure going to do it too.

Easier said than done.

As I made my desperately slow way across the stone face of the wall, I realised the skill and strength and self-confidence mom had just shown.

All the time mom's hand was now stretched out from the security of the gable towards me, inviting me onwards, promising me safety.

I've just got to do this, I told herself grimly, for mom and dad and me. Maybe for Greg too. I smiled to myself. Greg too.

Now the outstretched hand was inches from me, but the wind seemed to be rising and the moment had come to let go of my grip on the window lintel. To reach out.

Just as I was about to put my hand out, my right foot slipped a fraction, and in panic I looked down towards the drop below.

I heard mom's voice, whispering to me.

Nothing like that three hundred foot escarpment in Montana, honey. Nothing near as high at all. Hold on, get your hold back and we'll try again now. Come on, honey come to me. Give me a hand." The voice cool, insistent, confident.

I took a deep breath, as I had watched my mother do before, released my right hand grip. And reached out.

To feel a grip, as hard and secure as ever, I thought, and one which slid up and over my wrist, with two hands now, to pull me across and over onto the body of my mother lying partly across the slates of the roof and partly on the gable blocks themselves.

I gave a kick and a wrench and then I was over, held safe and secure for a moment by my mother. My ever-loving mother.

"Amy, I've had a quick look round up here. We're

going to go couple of steps down this gable edge, then out quietly across the slate roof to where I can see the hooked iron loops of a ladder. Hopefully that'll take us down to the ground at the back of the house. Then were home and dry, and we'll run like hell outa here. Got it?" And mom smiled again, as if all that had passed was as nothing. A minor incident
along life's path.

So easy when I look back on it. And it was over and past. Dealt with.

I remember taking a breath and nodding. Nothing to it.

SUNDAY

DATABOARD.

Day: **Sunday. Day 4.**

Weather   Strong wind from South to South East,
Watch: gusting 18-35 mph.

                   Overhead   65% cloud.
                   Forecast   Rising wind, Fair.

BoardWatch: 68 players 2-grouped.
                 First tee off 08.00 BST.
                 10min intervals.

Granger tee off 14.20 BST, match number 34.
Paired with Ritchie McAvon.

Big Board:

Player	Out	In	Total	Overall	Position
Round 1					
Granger	34	33	67	67	1
McAvon	35	34	69	69	2
Round 2					
Granger	36	33	69	136	1
McAvon	34	34	68	137	2
Round 3					
McAvon	36	33	69	206	1=
Granger	36	34	70	206	1=

CHAPTER FORTY SEVEN

In the pale cool half light of that July Sunday morning mom and I climbed down the iron ladder by the side of the house and made our way quickly out onto Links Road.

We were exhausted through the lack of sleep and the difficulties of our climb out the small window and along the tiny ledge to the crenellated edge of the roof.

I felt our brains too had had little rest and had been occupied with the turmoil of the day before. Not least also was the memory I had of the handgun the man in the room above had shown and the fact that any moment now he might discover our escape and come for us.

We hurried down Links Road and reached the place where the grandstand had been erected near the 18th tee. The only think I really noticed were two helicopters, parked away to our left on the Madras field area.

To my relief I noticed a security guard there. I went up to him and thankfully he recognised me as Granger's daughter. I played on this for all my worth, persuading him to let us slip under the crowd barrier rope and move a short distance onto the 18th fairway.

Mom and I made our way onto the Swilcan Bridge, crossing it and then moving on past the Jigger Inn we entered the Old Course Hotel by the rear door.

My room in the hotel was the only place of safety I could think of at the time though I had no key on me nor any means of id.

I must confess mom and I must have looked a bit dishevelled and tired as we approached the reception desk. I prayed that we would have no trouble getting the room key.

I smiled bravely at the receptionist who, thank the lord, smiled back at me, gave me a cheery 'Morning Miss Granger' and held out my room key without me even asking for it.

I nodded, unsure of making any conversation at all with her, turned with mom and we made our way across the lobby and on towards my room upstairs.

I say 'my room', but now it struck me that at this early time of the morning Greg would be there, fast asleep I thought.

We made it to our corridor without meeting anyone at all. I slipped the electronic key in the lock, withdrew it and turned the handle. The door opened first time.

We crept in quietly and for the first time in a while I felt safe. Mom must have felt the same, for she turned, hugged me, then indicated she was going to take a shower.

I kept the room light off and edged my way towards the bed.

There lay my beloved, my darling Greg. Never was I more pleased to see him.

I could now hear the sound of water from the shower as I bent over Greg and slowly, carefully kissed him awake. When he woke his eyes showed first confusion, then astonishment and lastly an absolute joy that I couldn't mistake.

He rolled out of bed and grabbed me.

We made love there and then. We didn't even make it to the bed. Strange the feeling of a carpet on your naked butt, yet never in my life had I felt more secure, more relieved and more loved than at that minute. Only the lump of my dead cellphone still in my elastic thigh bandage had momentarily delayed Greg.

After a while I heard the shower water being turned off and eventually mom came back into the room, wearing a bathrobe and looking thoughtful.

By this time I was sitting up in bed, wearing what I can't remember, and Greg was up, dressed and had drawn the curtains and Venetian blinds. My iPhone was back on charge too.

In a rush we told him our story, the grimness of the room we had been held captive in, the handgun, our escape and short journey to this room.

He explained what we already knew. That dad would sleep late today, have breakfast in his room, then later in the morning go along to his manager Mark Meekin's room where he and George Orr would go over his plan of attack on the course for this final round of the final day. Granger never allowed anything to break his concentration or his routine on a final Sunday, and least of all on the final round of an Open like this.

"So what do we do?" I asked.

It was mom who replied.

"We leave him be. Let him sleep. Let him have his normal routine, go to discuss things with Mark and George, then head off at his usual time to do his final practice and then make for the first tee. It would be nice for him to see us safe and well, but we're exhausted. We hardly slept at all last night the two of us so we'll have a sleep, enjoy a real breakfast for a change, then we'll see about things and meet up with dad later in the round."

"True," Greg agreed. "Granger comes first now. And anyway I don't like the sound of that man with the handgun. Who knows what he might do if or when he finds you two gone or if we turn up near Granger."

I hadn't thought of that. Sleep sounded good.

It was mom who made the final decision.

"Amy and I will get into this bed and take a nap. It would be great, Greg, if you ordered room service for us in a couple of hours time." She grinned. "Full English for me, with croissants, oatmeal bannocks, butter and heather honey, full grain rye toasted brown, with fresh orange juice and a pot of coffee."

I was astounded. All I could do was nod weakly and mutter, "Same for me."

I remember wondering if Greg had seen a vision of his future at that moment. He was a thoughtful man. He smiled and closed the blinds and curtains again.

Mom and I pulled up the cover, turned over and in seconds were fast asleep.

We awoke to the sound of the room service trolley coming in and then the curtains and blinds being drawn back once more.

Greg had done his job. The three of us sat down and I was astonished at just how much my mother and Greg consumed. I'm afraid I didn't do so well, but half an hour later we had finished.

Greg nodded towards my bedside table.

"I put your cellphone on charge. Looks like it's back to life again."

I grinned, picked up the phone and opened it.

The text message on it had been sent the night before, when my cellphone battery lay dead and useless.

Greg had gone out but had thoughtfully charged up my phone. What a kind, considerate young man. I was beginning to appreciate him more and more.

I opened the phone as quickly as I could, noticing the full bright light showing that my battery strength was now max.

The message, oddly enough was from that woman I had met briefly on the ramparts at Edinburgh Castle, so long before it seemed to me.

'Hi Amy

I have just locked the door to my third floor Edinburgh flat in Roxburgh's Close and walked down along the

Royal Mile. I will collect my morning coffee-to-go at Starbucks then cross the cobbles again to wait for the Air Enhance minibus as it heads up South Bridge to turn right then right again into the top of Cockburn St where it will pick me up.

What has this to do with anything, you're asking yourself, Amy. Bear with me. It is the most important time of my life coming up now.

I shall pull the sliding door aside, step up into the mini bus, nod vaguely at the other four employees inside, and chose as I always do the vacant rearmost seat.

I wonder if people now think of me as the Czech, Lisa Biric, or as the immigrant who was naturalised and spent more than 6 years in the US. No matter, Czech or American, they will have cause to remember me soon enough.

As the driver makes his way through the traffic to the west, towards Haymarket, and past the rear of Murrayfield Stadium on his daily journey, I know my thoughts will stray despite myself.

I have opened my Blackberry. Here at last is my story.

After 3 years in the States, a whirlwind courtship and a rapturous marriage I, Lisa Biric, settled down. I applied for and got US citizenship. And yet, 4 years later I changed from the loving, carefree wife and mother I had become. I had an adorable husband, Robert Brand and a smart young son Lucas. Robert ran a lucrative and well organized aero electronics company in Boston, Massachusetts on the outskirts of Logan Airport. In the summer of 2008 he had just extended his initial five-year contract with *Diack Technologies* for an additional new three-year contract.

And that that was where the trouble began, in August 2008, trouble for my husband and for his company that I also worked for as a flight electronics engineer and co-pilot.

My husband had extended his company loans, re-mortgaged our apartment and borrowed still more to take advantage of the continuing link with the Diack firm.

And in March 2009 it all went wrong.

The credit crunch, the bank crises, and the total downtown that year finally crippled my husband's company and forced him into bankruptcy. So easy to say, so easy to write down here. Just a few short words which can never do justice to the terrible, endless anxiety, depression and mental torture out small family suffered, all three of us. Do you understand? Or maybe you were outside all that awful trouble, above all those endless months of torture and despair.

I had to take an extra short term post as co-pilot and also as flight engineer with any company that was still flying. But in the end it had all come to nothing.

Diack himself had been cold, of no help, insisting that his company was dependent on the services my husband Brand had provided, that Diacks were now forced to sever their ties and look for a cheaper replacement aero electronics service provider than Brand.

So Brand's company struggled, twisted and turned for a way out, but eventually closed and what little family money we had left began to dwindle away. But that memory is not what has caused my rage.

I look out the minibus window as we move through Edinburgh, Through a different life it seems. Past PC World now and onwards towards the filling station at the Mayberry Junction. This all seems a fantasy life to me. Especially now. Especially today, now that my mind is made up and what will happen now will happen.

No, it was nor the penury and feeling of hopelessness that hardened my heart and firmed my resolve to take revenge on Alex Diack. It was what came next.

Though you cannot see them, you will forgive my tears here. The minibus is waiting at the Mayberry Junction lights for what seems an age, but now it's eventually crossing over onto Turnhouse Road itself. It will travel down into Turnhouse Airport, the private section of Edinburgh Airport.

I can feel my fists knotting in rage now as I remember that final, stunning blow to my life.

In what had seemed a generous action on the part of Diack, the company provided seats for my husband Robert and our son Lucas on a Diack private jet flying to L.A.

A godsend it seemed at the time. Though I myself still had two more weeks to fulfil on a short contract as co-pilot with a small air-ferry company at Logan, I was pleased that Robert and Lucas were going back to his father's place in LA. I would follow a couple of weeks later by whatever means I could.

But when the television that evening reported the crash of the Diack private jet, I could not bring myself to believe it.

Initial reports spoke only of the loss of the aircraft from LAX radar some 85 miles out from its destination. I didn't sleep. Next day I didn't go to work. That morning came graphic scenes of the crash site, high on a wooded hill. And bit by bit the grim finality of it all was revealed. There were no survivors. An electrical storm had affected the aircraft and its flight path, though what had actually caused the crash was not clear.

To me it was still not clear months after, but the absolute grief and misery at the loss of both my husband and son slowly and gave way to an ice-cold anger and blame.

I blamed myself, I blamed the deep recession, the banks and most of all I felt a burning rage against Diack, both the company and the man himself. Surely Diack must have kept the servicing of the aircraft up to date? I found out later, being in the job I was in, that in this matter the company had cut costs, as they had done in other areas.

I shake my head and wipe away even now the tears that come at the thought and memory of it. No matter what they say, time does not really heal. It just pastes over the memories and in an instant they can return.

After the unproven and concealed rumours of Diack's cutting of costs and the traumatic funeral, I came to a decision. Leaving Robert's father's home in L.A. I collected all the money I could scrape, beg or borrow. I bought a Greyhound bus ticket to Halifax, Nova Scotia, then flew under my maiden name and Czech passport in the co-pilot's seat of an air cargo jet to Manchester. Then on to Edinburgh.

The rest you will find out tomorrow.

I have left you my ring. You'll get it UPS Monday, together with a lovely jade necklace that was my mother's. If you wish the ring can be worn suspended on the necklace. The necklace has a message dating from way back. Look after the ring and necklace and think of me sometimes.

Farewell and God bless.

Lisa Boric Brand.'

I glanced across at mom, wondered what the day would bring and decided to wait and think a bit more before we took any decisions.

I went for a shower, Greg took his turn after me, and mom washed up again.

When I got back to the cleared breakfast table, Greg hurriedly closed down the laptop he'd been using. At the time I thought it was just politeness on his part, but it turned out later he hadn't wanted me to see the negative headlines many of the online newspapers were giving dad.

"Greg," I said at last, "I'm not going to hide here in our room and let those guys who kidnapped us determine what we'll do now. I'm going to go out, find that house and see what we can do."

Greg was learning fast. He seemed to know who was boss. Or at least, when to let people believe they were boss, let them have their way when need be, both me and my mother.

"Right," he replied. "Let's do it. What d'you say mom?"

I blinked. An alpha male kowtowing? And 'mom'?

Or was Greg cleverer than I thought?

Half an hour later we were out.

CHAPTER FORTY EIGHT

It seemed a different kind of day. Cloudier at times, with definitely much more wind, coming in sudden and at times violent gusts.

We found the house we'd been kept in. Of course there were more people around now. The stands were full and The Links road was packed.

And there was a policewoman outside the door to the house.

How could that be? How had the police been brought into it and exactly to that house? I checked. The window up above was the same, but unshuttered now. The downstairs curtained windows were the same. And the front door had not changed. It was definitely the same place.

I found out later that what had happened in the meantime was that in the flat the Chinese man Wei had come upstairs about seven that morning to check on mom and me, found us gone, the window prised open and of course must have panicked and fled at once.

Realising the game was up, he had rapidly used his cellphone to summon the others in his group, and leaving only the four PHaSR operatives to carry on to the bitter end, had ordered everyone to the two helicopters they had on stand-by on Madras field.

Wei and his group had waited impatiently and anxiously till they had lifted off.

We went up to the policewoman at the house door, who explained curtly but politely that the recent tenant had left, been involved in an accident and was gravely injured.

I explained who we were, mentioned that we could probably identify the tenant and could we help.

In minutes a police car with motorcycle escort had arrived and taken all three of us off, sirens wailing, through the crowds and down along the Scores at breakneck pace.

We stopped next the Castle, inside a ring of police vehicles and three ambulances.

We were shepherded out, across the roadway and down a steep path that normally led to a small beach and long fingers of rock below.

And there I saw a horrific sight.

A police inspector checked who we were, then explained. "Two helicopters carrying the man you know and four others, took off this morning from the Madras Field helipad across from the Old Course Hotel.

Seems these choppers had been commissioned by

someone called Alex Diack. I think you know him?"

I nodded, gazing in horror at the wreckage in front of us. The inspector continued.

"The two choppers took off, as I said, and flew out towards St Andrews Bay. They then turned south and came down the coast just beside the Scores."

He paused and checked his notepad.

"Seems they were both taking the five passengers ultimately to Edinburgh Airport.

We have a wind this morning, as you've seen, a horrible, gusting, swirling wind but they must have risked the flight nevertheless.

They came down the coastline, keeping still fairly low, perhaps to give the passengers a last look at St Andrews. Who knows.

Anyway, just above the castle there must have been a sudden upsurge of the south east wind up the cliff face, then an equally sudden downdraft. Witnesses say one of the helicopters was blown down and into the other, the rotors clashing. The choppers tangled, heeled over and both crashed into the rocks and beach here."

He paused and looked at us.

"I'm afraid there are no survivors. However if you could ID any of the victims it would help us greatly. That is, if you're up to it. It's not a pretty sight, I think."

I didn't know what to feel. On the one hand, if it was the guy who'd held us prisoners, threatened us indirectly with a gun, and had helped to try and coerce or blackmail dad, then he deserved everything he'd got.

"Let's do it." It was mom who made the decision.

So we went down the slope and across the sand to the rocks a little way.

There were five stretchers laid out, with a blanket over each.

The inspector led us over to the nearest one.

"Ready?"

Mom and I nodded, and the top of the blanket was pulled back.

The face was battered and blood streaked. But unmistakably our Chinese man from the room. The ears alone would almost have identified him.

I nodded, mom nodded, and we turned away.

We recognised none of the others.

CHAPTER FORTY NINE

The news headlines and reports that Greg read on his mobile that Sunday morning did not make good reading. Not if you were a Granger fan that was.

Granger: Thursday 67, Friday 69, Saturday 70.
Total 206.
McAvon: Thursday 69, Friday 68, Saturday 69
Total 206.

McAvon had overhauled Granger, gaining in experience as they went round the Old Course.
On that reckoning McAvon today would overtake Granger, even in the gusty conditions that now prevailed. Some said McAvon would do that, not in spite of but because of the conditions that now prevailed, especially as McAvon was so accustomed to such weather over his

home course, Pebble Beach.

On Granger's insistence he, Greg, George and Mark had gone to the hotel breakfast parlour.

As he sat there at a window table with Granger, Greg did his best to keep those reports away from Granger. Not that Granger ever paid much attention to newspaper or online articles anyway, as Greg well knew.

Granger made up his own mind about his performance, discussed it with George Orr and Mark Meekin, then formed his plan of action for the day accordingly.

Only rarely did he show signs of emotion, weakness or self doubt, and Greg admired him greatly for this. Especially considering the trials and tribulation that seemed to have beset Granger recently and in particular over this last week, Greg thought.

On Wednesday past, the practice day, Granger had shot a poor score, not surprising after the Tuesday night rigged murder scene at the Swilcan bridge, then the e-mail of the following morning warning of the consequences to his wife Laura.

On Thursday, despite it all, on a calm day with no wind or rain Granger had shot a 4 under par round from his 08.31 start and led the field.

Friday he had posted a 6-under round after his 13.50 start. This despite continuing harassment from those who held Laura captive and continuing and growing pursuit from Ritchie McAvon against a background of benign weather from the notoriously fickle Old Course in the 150th Anniversary of the Open.

Saturday from a 13.50 start Granger had wavered a little,

carding a respectable 7 under but had been ominously overtaken by McAvon, though the immediate field behind now trailed further behind. And the wind had risen a little, even if the weather had still held.

Greg thumbed over to the first online report for that morning.

"With a wind of 18 to 35 mph. now and the challenge of coming from behind if he can manage it at all, Granger would seem to be second favourite today or even worse, and may be forced into some high tariff shots. What's more, there will be moisture now in the greens making up in difficulty for the straightforward pin positions today. And as always, somebody could come out of the pack and shoot a good number, but their short game will have to be good and shots off the tee are always an issue in a facing wind through the back nine.

The day will be a test for the top eight favourites and the wind will cause problems for most.

This may not be the case however for both of the final pair, McAvon and Granger, as both are familiar with windswept links-type courses.

Though Granger has the advantage of the youngster in experience overall and of course in the British Open in particular, can any golfer achieve three Open wins so soon the one after the other? Especially as Granger has seemed distracted and under the weather emotionally at times lately.

McAvon has youth, vitality and a 'nothing to lose attitude' in his favour and if he tackles this final round with the flamboyancy and flair he has shown at Pebble

Beach and indeed over the previous three days here at St Andrews, then he can retain his lead over Granger and indeed increase on it."

Greg winced as he read this and quickly thumbed his screen over to other commentators and news reports. But not a single one seemed to differ from the first analysis.

He quickly shut down his Blackberry, put it away, and hurried to make conversation with Granger. Talking about anything, anything at all to keep Granger's mind off his captive wife and daughter, the threat to his own standing, and the worry of the day ahead.

The last thing Greg remembered seeing as they left the dining room was the glaring headline of a Sunday paper one guest was holding up high:

'Rookie McAvon Now Odds-on Favourite for St Andrews Open.'

And another:

'Granger trails by 2. Looking lacklustre over his finishing four holes yesterday.'

And just as they left by the restaurant door:

'Ritchie McAvon set to be favourite in dramatic finish to 150th OPEN'

' McAvon on top of the world. Supremely confident of his chances on this big final day, despite forecast of overcast skies with occasional bright spells and winds gusting from the south west.'

Greg hurried Granger out before he could see the remainder of that report which Greg had already skimmed over at the breakfast table:

'*There is sure to be a huge following for the last 68 players today, and especially for those really in contention; according to the Big Scoreboard, the pairs in the final 8 matches.*'

'*Nothing different to what I'm used to at Pebble Beach*' *McAvon told this golf correspondent yesterday.* '*Let the weather come and do its worst or best. I'm up for it and more than a match for the more experienced guys like Granger.*'

Looks like today he could be right. Most of the others thought to be front runners have now fallen back a bit and will struggle to match McAvon.

Only Granger can possibly hold him and with each minute now Granger's looking less and less likely to manage that. His prospects of a third Open win look slim.'

'*McAvon and Granger are paired together and out last today. Match 34 at 14.20.*'

CHAPTER FIFTY

Diack slept the sleep of the successful, rising at ten.
Reception informed him the Air Enhance airfreight rep
had collected the Cadillac the evening before.
After a leisurely lunch Diack strolled round to Turnhouse.
Things were going well.
He then walked over to where his silver Learjet stood
alone on its hard stand outside the conglomerates Air
Enhance hangar.

The engineers and Learjet maintenance men were now
fussing round the aircraft. So Diack took time off to
e-mail his villa in the Bahamas on his Blackberry Bold
to advise them of his coming. Perhaps he would even
pay off the mortgage on the villa outright now.
Life was good.
He decided not to read the Sunday Open headlines yet

on his cellphone but to delay the pleasure of finding out the winner until he was safely on his way out over the Atlantic.

He had planned well and thought of everything.

He sat at ease in the leather chair in the Air Enhance lounge, idly watching incoming aircraft on final approach from the northeast to the main Edinburgh Airport runway. The wind had picked up but was still nothing to concern him.

With his coffee Diack was given a copy of *Time* magazine and he flicked through the pages as the clock hands crept round.

A business-like Air Enhance executive entered the lounge, took his briefcase for him and escorted him to a few short steps across the hard standing and up the stairs into the waiting Learjet, to go through the pilot's briefing with him.

The female co-pilot and flight engineer was also on hand to share the briefing. For a fraction of a second Diack thought he might just have seen the woman before but instantly dismissed it from his thoughts. After all he had been around pilots and mechanics and engineers now for the past five years and more of his life. Faces and people came and went, changing jobs, changing companies, losing jobs, moving on. Their comings and goings were not really his affair.

Diack and his co-pilot completed the pre-flight prep, performed the onboard and final checks, while the co-pilot took any last minute incoming messages. Diack himself flew the jet off from Edinburgh's runway, with Lisa as co-pilot.

Rising steeply from the main runway, Diack climbed to 10,000', confirmed his course with Air Traffic Control then turned out to sea just north of Ireland. He switched to autopilot and autoreport and took off his headphones, settling the Learjet into its flight path, out north of Ireland and into its Atlantic routing.

At this point Diack handed over the controls to the co-pilot and announced he would take a sleep. He asked the co-pilot to waken him to tune into the final stages of the British Open on the radio and finally fly the aircraft down into Boston Logan.

What a pleasant smile she has, Diack thought to himself as he drifted into his nap. And somehow or other, a familiar face, though he just couldn't remember from where or when.

CHAPTER FIFTY ONE

George Orr glanced across at his boss and partner Jack Granger as they headed up towards the ninth.

The view was great, as it had been over the last four crucial days.

Back down the course Orr saw the holes and fairways that had been so treacherous for some. And far off, the skyline of the old town of St Andrews, windblown and crowned with clouds now.

A swirling east to south-east wind chopped the North Sea stretching off to the right, with the shoreline of Angus way in the distance.

Nearer at hand the sandbanks and swirls of the Eden flowed, curling round the top far end of the Old Course. And across the River Eden lay the expanse of Leuchars airfield, with all those parked jets and other planes ready for the off. Tonight, tomorrow, or who knew when, once the championship and all the festivities had finished.

Didn't look at all like he and Granger would be sharing in them. Pity. Jack had started off so well and the media had had him slated for a win. Some week.

But now McAvon had done as many had predicted. He was about to card a completed outward nine holes of 35, two shots under Granger's probable 37.

Orr paid little attention to McAvon. It wasn't McAvon he was worried about. He had years on his side. It was Granger he was thinking of.

He had heard this called a gentleman's game. It was, in some ways. In others it was the most fiendish, cold blooded, calculating battle he knew.

Across from the group of spectators to his right, Greg told me later, Orr looked at the ring of faces sitting in the 9th Hole grandstand. Sitting, waiting, expecting miracles. And most of the time getting none.

The only face he recognised apparently was Greg.

But then miracles do happen. And indeed a miracle happened there and then.

To one side of Greg, Orr saw two faces he recognised. Mine and my mom's.

McAvon had already pitched his ball up to within two feet of the flag. Granger had laid up onto the green, 10 feet or so from the pin. He was now stretching out a hand to Orr for his putter.

But George Orr's eyes and mind were elsewhere. On us. I saw dad ask Orr for the putter again and move towards him, maybe just a tad annoyed at George's loss of concentration.

Then dad followed Orr's gaze. And I saw his eyes meet ours. Mom's and mine.

From that moment, from that hole, dad, Jack Granger, was galvanised. He was electric, ecstatic. A man reborn. And what a golfer!

Whenever he looked for us and saw us, he beamed. Boy did he smile! And boy did he turn out some golf. McAvon could not have known what had come over Granger, till no doubt someone explained to him that Granger's wife was back. Nobody really seemed to have missed me too much, but I knew I'd done my part.

And so we skipped back home along the back nine. Towards the 18th.

CHAPTER FIFTY TWO

The 18th hole at St. Andrews looks straightforward enough. Leastways it does still to me, a mere female, even if I am the daughter of Jack Granger. After all, any good pro worth his salt can drive that final green from the tee, I'd have thought. Par 4, 357 yards.

And yet that Sunday the 18th could be something else, especially if you were level with your opponent and everything depended on the result of just this one hole. Playing into a gusting 18-35 miles per hour wind from the south east it is even more so.

For Granger it could have been at any rate. But the reappearance of his wife Laura and me had made a new man of him.

Granger to tee off first.

And so on the 18th tee he breathed deeply and concentrated.

CHAPTER FIFTY THREE

That same Sunday afternoon 1200 miles out over the Atlantic at 31,000 feet, Lisa Brand was listening to the radio station she had tuned to. She had checked the automated flight reporting system up to then and was satisfied all was in order.

The first item of news to catch her attention should have been immensely satisfying to her. Yet strangely it wasn't. The business news section that day reported that an American company had just declared Chapter 11. The bankrupt company was *Diack Technologies*.

A second report was of a double helicopter crash with fatalities in east Scotland.

The third report was from the sports desk. The commentary of the final stages of the British Open Golf Championship, about to come to a conclusion at St

Andrews.

Lisa switched the flight controls of the chartered Learjet to auto-pilot, checked again that the auto flight indication and report system were functioning and walked aft from the cockpit.

In the cabin she stopped and stood looking down at the sleeping form of Eric Diack. He lay at peace, it seemed, sleeping comfortably on the same bench seat inside which the kidnapped Laura Granger had been drugged and hidden during her abduction from Boston to Leuchars and then to the gabled house on The Links road in St Andrews.

Lisa thought back to the events of the previous two days. Her flight prep for the hired Learjet's journey to Boston Logan had gone well.

Unknown to anyone at that time save Alex Diack, Wei was to take a scheduled KLM flight from Edinburgh to Amsterdam Schipol, connecting there to the KLM non-stop outward leg to Shanghai where he would spend a year enjoying his winnings.

There would be no other passengers on the Learjet, Diack had informed Lisa. She was unaware that Diack had taken care of his team of watchers at the Open, Sam Wei having told to pay them all off and organise their early departure from the Old Course on the Saturday or Sunday, well before the last hour of the final round, apart from the four final laser cameramen.

So Diack and she were alone in the chartered Learjet.

Now she stood at Diack's side, holding a small box in

her hand and looking down at the sleeping man.

She began to speak, softly at first, almost to herself, certainly not loud enough to waken Diack. As she spoke her voice grew firmer and with that hint of anger and yet sorrow that had sustained and driven her all those months.

" My Robert Brand was an engineer, a family man, a hard working man who had worked first at an aircraft company that he left and slowly built up his own small company. Built it into a respected and skilled firm with connections to *Diack Technologies*. But one day you saw your chance and offered my husband a contract. And you encouraged Bob Brand to go and borrow extensively from the banks in order to fulfil this contract with you. To do this he had to extend himself. Perhaps it was your powers of persuasion, perhaps it was his sight of a real and prosperous future, for that company of his, for himself, for his family. Who knows? Was it greed? Was it profit? Was it achievement? Good or bad? Who knows? The dividing line is fine.

At any rate, he borrowed, heavily. And that hideous financial collapse came.

You, Alex Diack, refused to help him or to extend the contract time on the work you required.

And so my husband's company dwindled, and suffered, and collapsed, and my husband became penniless. Fool that he was, you might say and turn away. Business is a hard taskmaster.

But I hated the bankers, those financial wizards who had enticed us and flattered us and smiled on us with extended hands in the good days, and now shunned and avoided us. As if we had not been, did not now exist.

And then, in a seeming gesture of goodwill and hope, as part of a pitiful bankruptcy settlement, you, Alex Diack, offered one of your remaining Company's aircraft to fly my penniless Bob Rand and our darling young son Lucas. A flight to take the two, my two, back to stay with Bob's mother in Los Angeles. A refuge? A new start? Or another period of hopelessness, for so many now were unemployed and unemployable in that horrible recession.

So my man ended up in poverty.

And you washed your hands of him, forgot about him. A man who had not only been a good provider for your company but also a friend of yours over several years.

I have never forgotten nor forgiven you, Alex Diack, for the day you deserted my husband and I lost him and my only son Lucas, when your plane crashed on its final stage to L.A. You had cut costs and pared away at what you saw as excesses. And maintenance of your aircraft was one way you and your company cut corners.

But negligence was never proved in that crash, nor ever even mentioned. And you and your fancy lawyers smiled and walked away from it all.

Life without these two loved ones has proved unbearable and potentially suicidal for me. But I had stayed while they flew off to L.A. I stayed and earned my keep with a small aircraft company near Boston, as an onboard engineer and co-pilot.

After the first few hard weeks I vowed to weep no more, picked myself up, steeled myself and worked out my plan over all these months. I have devised it and carried it out to this day.

Working as flight engineer and co-pilot on the Learjet at Air Enhance at Edinburgh Turnhouse I have completed my final preparations for this day, preparations I have made for just one Learjet. Your Learjet. This Learjet. And now contained in part of this plane and in this little box here in my hand. This box I painstakingly built over the months at Air Enhance and in that old flat on Edinburgh's Royal Mile."

She stopped and looked down again at the sleeping Diack.

Quite why he wanted to hear the Open result and at this particular time she didn't know, nor did she care. But then he was the boss and the pilot in charge and had instructed her to wake him for that moment.

CHAPTER FIFTY FOUR

Lisa put the electronic box now in her flying suit pocket, shook Diack gently awake, and watched as he gradually came to, raising himself on one elbow and smiling sleepily up at her as he rubbed his eyes.

He was at peace, she saw, and yet strangely eager, with a mounting anticipation as he swung his legs off the couch-bed and got up.

He looked up at her and said.

"It's funny you know. I have this feeling I know you from some where. Do I know you? Should I know you?"

Lisa smiled and turned away from him.

She had tuned the radio into the BBC Overseas Service and now she turned up the volume for him, seating herself just opposite and behind him.

The announcer continued the BBC live transmission from St Andrews and Lisa watched as Diack's face lit up in anticipated joy.

Yet Lisa barely paid attention to the radio as she gathered herself for her final decision. She could either do as she had planned to for ten months, or forgive, forget and let life roll on as if nothing much happened. And anyway, she thought to herself. Six months, a year, ten years from now who would remember, who would care, to whom would it matter? And yet she believed there was such a thing as justice, rude or primitive though it might be.

"And now the final hole of what could be, should be the final round at the Open today.

McAvon and Granger are now level as they stand on this tee, with the Tom Morris 18th fairway ahead of them. Of course, if they tie, then they will have to go to a playoff. Pebble Beach's fabulous rookie, Ritchie McAvon and two time holder of the British Open, Jack Granger, have battled it out over this 4th and final round today, in spite of lowering skies and a wind gusting at times from 18 to 35 miles per hour over the back 9 holes of this famous old course.

To recap, Granger in fact carded a 37 over the front nine holes, two over McAvon's 35. Though over the back nine things have changed"

To Lisa, Diack's face was a picture of relief and joy, yet some concern.

Diack turned to her.

"I had a bet on the rookie finishing in the final," he shouted out. "I knew he would do it! Those years McAvon spent at Pebble Beach have proved their worth now. He's no stranger to a windy links course. And he has the strength and optimism of youth over Granger."

The commentary continued.

"McAvon still leads, but somehow or other Granger has seemed revitalised and come on like a storm from behind.

Diack fell silent as the announcer read out the final scores.

"The 18th hole, as always, will prove the decider. With the demon of the Valley of Sin and that killer of an 18th green up ahead both men are level pegging at 68 strokes each. There's no other competitor in contention.

Since he overhauled McAvon, playing over the sheds, up past the Old Course Hotel then sinking a wonderful long range 18 yard putt on the 17th green, Granger will now play off first on the 18th tee."

The commentator paused and in the cabin Diack's face glowed with excitement. Now he was rubbing his hands furiously in anticipation.

The commentator resumed.

"With a strong south east wind in his face, Granger seems set to play down the right of the fairway, past the Swilcan Bridge and over Granny Clark's Wynd. An odd decision, I must say."

Again there came a pause in the commentary.

"He'll land short taking that route, I think, and perilously close to the out-of-bound on The Links road. And even if he makes it, Granger's next shot from there will require all his patience, bravery and skill.

It looks like Ritchie McAvon has selected the opposite

route, hitting with his 3 iron longer out left, almost towards the 1st fairway, opting for distance and then trusting to his fabled accuracy."

CHAPTER FIFTY FIVE

Granger avoided looking at the favourite now, Ritchie McAvon and gazed instead away up the fairway towards the final flag. He selected a three wood. His caddy George gazed up at him, opened his mouth to speak in protest, then quickly shut his mouth again and prepared to face the worst.

Granger had decided on a high tariff shot. The kind George Orr dreaded and hated.

Jack was about to try something exceptional. Something that his caddy George Orr had simply shaken his head at. Something that Granger remembered being told about in a conversation with one of the locals.

It would be an exceptional shot. Or damn him as a fool for ever more. A shot that would either make or break him. Yet with his wife and daughter beside him now, he felt once more the old balance within him of cold objective choice and daredevil all-or-nothing skill.

Jack Granger steeled himself and rehearsed the shot in his head.

First he would use a three wood only, to keep the ball to no more than 20 to 35 feet high. And he would not drive the green, nor line up his shot straight ahead, as the hole seemed to demand, but down the right, near the Links Road.

In fact, he would choose to do two more things that would scandalise the pundits. Let them watch now, and admire, or jeer.

Granger waited for just a moment more, when the gusting wind seemed to have reached its strength, then he struck. He watched, and with him hundreds, thousands, perhaps millions watched, as did Ritchie McAvon, as the ball was punched out into the wind. It scarcely rose at all, and seemed too far out to the right. In fact, after crossing over to one side of the Swilcan bridge, it swung out in an arc to the right.

When it cleared Granny Clark's Wynd the parabola seemed to balloon out more to the right, till Granger's ball swung out from the fairway and coursed on, actually out of bounds and above the white fence and heads of the watchers, over the narrow reach of The Links road itself.

CHAPTER FIFTY SIX

The commentary in the Learjet came out loud and clear now.

"Granger's ball has reached a spot nearly opposite the gap in the buildings beside *Rusacks Hotel*. But now something miraculous has happened, folks. Something that Granger no doubt had sensed and grasped and counted on.

A side gust, billowing out from that gap in the buildings by the Rusacks Hotel, has seized his ball and swept it. Swept it miraculously, demoniacally back to the left, dumping it unceremoniously back onto the fairway, and rolling it neatly up on to a little knoll. Where it has come to rest, sitting proud on the very crest of a mound of fairway turf, with a clear and straight uphill path to the 18th pin.

The crowd have given a great sigh of relief, then a huge burst of applause, and whistles have broken out. Good for Granger that. He took one hell of a risk, but it's paid off. He's now got an approach shot up the green, then at most two putts, perhaps even the chance of just one putt, though the pin is set up to the back right on a sloping green."

Dad later told me his thoughts on that 18th fairway and green.

Chance it! Work it all out in your head and then if you can do it all and succeed you're home and dry. And remember, you lucky old fool who now has his wife and his daughter back. This final hole's a wonderful moment for you. You'll relive it all your life. No matter what.

CHAPTER FIFTY SEVEN

Now back on the tee, Granger and Orr watched as McAvon pushed his tee into the grass, exactly half way between the two markers.

"Wonder what's going through McAvon's mind?" Orr whispered to Granger. "He's not going to attempt to follow your line and head off up the right. Too much of a risk. He's going to play the more conventional shot. He's a young guy after all, and perhaps he'll choose to chance his luck later.

He must be careful. He's seen how you attacked the hole. But he has to watch it. If the wind catches his drive, if he's a fraction off centre or a fraction too lofted with his strike, that demon of a wind will take him hell knows where!"

The crowd had fallen silent again.

They watched as McAvon conferred with his caddie,

threw up into the air a blade or two of grass that the wind whirled away behind him, then selected a 3 iron.

So McAvon was going to follow Granger's example in one respect and make no attempt to drive the green. Granger smiled to himself.

McAvon breathed in deeply several times, eyed up the fairway once more, then stepped up to the tee. And made his strike.

His ball also did not rise high. McAvon was playing it safe with the wind at a lower level, as Granger had done. But McAvon, despite his experience on the links fairways of Pebble Beach, kept to the centre path, his drive arcing out further than Granger's had, but to the left and nearer the 1st fairway, and to some extent rising higher.

His ball cleared Granny Clark's Wynd and drove on. The power and ease in his drive was there for all to see.

But as the ball flew, there came sudden dramatic gust in the wind and McAvon's ball carried on, rising ever so slightly, to swing at the last to the left. And landed into that hollow, the awkward hollow just before the Valley of Sin.

On that drive McAvon, whether through relative inexperience or just plain bad luck, had placed his shot closer to the green that dad's but with not such a clear shot now to it.

There came a pause in the commentary.

"Looks like McAvon could gain some 30 yards here over Granger."

Again there was a pause, and Diack's tension yet glee was obvious to Lisa as she fingered her small electronic box. Not yet, she told herself.

The commentary paused again.

CHAPTER FIFTY EIGHT

The commentary on the Learjet's radio resumed.

"Granger to chip first. As I said, he has about 30 yards disadvantage to the pin over McAvon.
Another pause.
"Looks like Granger's trying to asses the wind strength, but it's gusting here and you can never be sure of choosing the right moment to strike. It's a real nightmare of a hole this, the 18th. Always has been.
He's addressing the ball now. Not much of a back swing, I think and he must watch the fencing up the right of this fairway. The *Rusacks Hotel* and the row of houses along The Links road stand behind him as Granger waits to choose his moment."
Yet another pause in the radio commentary.

Mom and I stood not far from dad as he prepared to make

that second shot.

I watched him breath deeply again, then swing, and chip towards the pin, keeping more to a chip and chase than anything.

His ball finished on the green, 11 feet below the pin.

Two putts now to finish on a par four, I thought, squeezing mom's hand tight, two putts, provided he doesn't either undershoot or overshoot the pin and roll drastically back down. The pin position was alright, though the sloping green was tricky and the wind, now gusting now calmer, didn't help at all.

Again Granger and Orr watched with interest as McAvon and his caddie discussed the probabilities.

"McAvon has to assume I can hole my 11 foot putt," Granger murmured, more to himself than to George Orr. Granger was now totally unaware of the crowd near him or round the hole ahead. And yet he turned and looked for me and mom. And both of us saw for that fleeting second just how stressed dad's face was.

"We've got to get him to concentrate and relax as much as he can," mom whispered in my ear. I nodded.

But what could we do?

Over the Learjet radio there came a roar.

"Granger has chipped. Looks ok but the wind could take it any moment and swing it out way left towards the Valley of Sin, those horrible sunken dips and hollows that are a golfer's nightmare and death."

Lisa waited. Now, or not yet? She asked herself.

She waited, watching Diack's face, his anxiety and yet excitement.

"Granger has been lucky. His chip has landed some 13 feet on the green and 11 feet from the pin. A two putt at the most, maybe even a single stroke to sink it.

A crowd of well-wishers are waving to him from The Links road. Granger's still looking anxiously around the crowd. Can't quite see who he's checking for but Granger seems almost to be losing some of his calm and control. A crucial moment for him now. A moment of decision.

"And now for McAvon. He's seen Granger make the green, not far on it but not too far from the pin. McAvon must attempt to clear the Valley of Sin and play for the green. The wind is blowing more across his approach than it was for Granger as McAvon waits and judges his moment."

Another breathless pause in the radio commentary and Diack clenched his fists still tighter.

"McAvon has struck it well. Hard and high, in an attempt to clear the hollows and traps of the Valley of Sin then get some spin and hold when his ball hits the green. He is right on line for the green and the pin. Right on line.

"But now the gusting wind has dropped, allowing his ball to drift even higher and further on, and oh no! His ball has held but landed higher up the green, 13 feet beyond the pin! And a downhill lie.

Both men have taken two strokes so far and there's no telling who will clinch this final hole.

Granger has taken his putter and is waiting to line up and address his ball, talking with his caddy George Orr.

That group of well-wishers I mentioned before, on the Links road beside Granger, have now turned away and are moving back down The Links road. I can make them out better now. My god! One of them seems to be, hold on a minute while we check."

In the plane the hiss of static ran on for a few seconds.

"Yes! One of them is in fact his wife, Laura!"

Lisa saw Diack start. His face turned pale, then contorted with fury.

The commentator's voice broke into their thoughts again.

"Way back in May Laura Granger seemed to have walked out on Granger, left him and settled elsewhere. But now, here she is, waving and shouting to Granger. He's seen her and is staring at her again! And I can now confirm that the others beside Mrs Granger are her daughter, Amy, Amy's fiancé Greg Wells, and Granger's manager Mark Meekin. What a group! They're cheering Granger on and yet gesticulating, turning away and pointing back down the fairway.

One of them, I'm sure it's his wife, seems to be making a sign of prayer with her palms together. And now her daughter Amy is making a double thumbs up sign. I'm not sure what that all means but Granger seems reassured now.

"Granger is waiting now for McAvon to putt. Granger's 17 feet on the green, 11 to the pin. Still into the wind. Direct into the wind. Uphill putt.

He's waiting for McAvon to play first. McAvon, to recapitulate, lies 13 feet above the pin, up on the slope, with a downhill putt.

McAvon is taking an age, and must realise he needs a wonder shot if he's to share this final hole and force a playoff now! But he's produced magical shots here this week at St Andrews, time and time again."

CHAPTER FIFTY NINE

I didn't really know at that point if dad had understood our gestures.

Encouraging him as we did, but moving away and giving him time and reassurance to concentrate on that final hole was all mom and I could think of. Yet it had its dangers. We made our way back down The Links road. We couldn't bear to turn and watch. We knew his concentration now should be total. No distractions needed. And anyway the crowd would let us know what had happened.

In the Learjet Diack was hunched forward, completely unaware of Lisa, totally focussed on the radio commentary.

"Here goes McAvon. His 7 iron in the wind was good. He's well on the green, but above the pin. 13 feet above it, with the green fence and Hamilton Hall right behind him as he will take his next putt. Downhill and slightly on a sideways slope, but nothing he's not managed before, on similar courses or at Pebble Beach where he performed so well two months ago.

Granger is waiting. Has picked up and will replace his ball.

McAvon's taking an age to address the ball. Don't blame him. So much depends on this. Difficult downhill putt though. And that wind! You just can't tell when it will slacken off or gust. If McAvon misses the hole, the ball may continue on down. He's got to sink it."

To Diack listening in the plane, the next few seconds seemed an eternity, with just the soft hiss of the radio channel to show that anything was going on, when in fact Diack's future and life were in the balance.

A slight patch of interference clouded the radio reception and Diack grimaced. Lisa watched his face and tensed too, but for another reason. The moment must now come, she thought.

"He's done it. McAvon has chosen his moment and putted! His ball is online for the hole, maybe allowing for a slight right-to-left. It's holding, holding, holding. And on line.

And it's there, right up to the hole."

Another final agonising pause in the commentary.

And then:

"But oh no! It has agonizingly lipped the cup! Lipped the cup and slid on 9 inches past. Looked like it was a cert, then at the last minute failed to turn, and just caught the lip of the cup and slid on! Would you believe it!

McAvon certainly can't!

It's taken a while for the hubbub to die down and the crowd to recover again. At last there's silence once more as we wait. Now for Granger to putt."

Diack had slumped in the pilot's chair, limp, yet still with some ray of hope to his face, Lisa thought.

"Granger's chance now. An incredible putt, at that distance, uphill and in those conditions! Granger has replaced his ball, about 11 feet now from the pin. Almost a straight lie. Just a slight draw to the left.

"Now, what can Granger do? 11 feet from the pin. Uphill. Almost a straight line. Just the slightest of draws maybe to the left. Unmissible, you would say. And yet …

He's had a word with his caddy. Granger is now heedless of the crowd. He has made up his mind. He's chosen his line and is addressing the ball.

You can hear a pin drop here. I wonder what has happened to the rest of the Granger family? For that matter, I wonder what's going through Granger's mind? Does he have a dilemma? Heaven knows, the shot itself is hard enough, without the tension, the stress of an Open Championship, and such an occasion as this in addition. Final day, final hole. This to win. And millions watching, listening, wondering, wagering on the outcome.

He must hole this putt to draw and avoid a playoff if he wants this championship title.

There's hardly a murmur to be heard here as the crowd and the cameras wait and watch.

McAvon, his caddy and Orr are absorbed. I'm certain Granger hasn't noticed that his wife and daughter and her fiancé have walked back down to a spot near the Swilcan Bridge.

Granger has decided on his line. He's hesitating, judging the wind it seems. But with this devil of a hole and the tension you never can tell! "

Diack had cupped his head in his hands and hardly seemed able to listen any more. Lisa had her hand in her pocket. She was swaying slightly now from side to side, in a gentle, mesmerising-like motion behind Diack.

"Granger has putted. His ball is rolling slowly now up to the pin. Not quite online perhaps? He seems to be allowing for the slightest of draws.

The very slightest of gusts of wind has come up.

Granger's ball is... Is coming up to the pin. A vague groan from the crowd. The ball appears to be heading just past the hole, half an inch or so to the right. And the wind and the slope may carry it away.

"We're all waiting now. In the distance, back near the Swilcan I can see Laura Granger, Amy, and Greg Wells clutching each other and waiting, waiting and hoping as Granger waits and watches this ball.

The ball's tracking out right, out right still. Now its coming in. In. Still in. If it misses, Granger too may end up rolling back down the slope, I fear!

No, it's bending! The wind is carrying it! Favouring it! Granger's putt is drawing to the hole. It's in! Granger has done it!

"A thunderous roar has broken out from this final hole

gallery!   Granger is home, one single shot below his rival!   Just when we thought we might have a playoff for the final of the 150th Anniversary of the Open Golf Championship at St Andrews!

An astounding event with an unbelievable finish!

Jack Granger is for the third time Open Champion of this great event in this wonderful, historic setting!"

CHAPTER SIXTY

"A massive group of photographers and tv crews has surrounded McAvon and Granger at the edge of this final green. Yet I can see Laura, Amy and their little group far off now down The Links road. Why should they be there at such a momentous occasion? I don't understand it!

It seems as if they are heading for the Old Course Hotel. Yet wait. I think they're making a deviation.

Just someway down the road, Laura seems to be having a word with two course officials. Yes. She and her group are stepping up and over, on to the edge of the 18th fairway and making their way to the left.

I'm not sure what is going on. No, wait. It appears now that they are all heading for the little bridge. The little stone Swilcan Bridge.

And now, at last, Jack Granger has broken free of the crowd of media folk and well wishers up at the 18th green. George Orr has pointed out to him his wife and the others, standing on the Swilcan Bridge, waving and yelling to him.

The camera crews and others have cottoned on to what's happening! They're chasing Granger back down the side of the 18th fairway, where Granger has now made his way up into the arms of his wife and daughter and the others. A laughing, crying, crowd, as the cameras record and the crowds roar their approval.

A momentous time, a momentous day."

CHAPTER SIXTY ONE

Lisa's final moment had come.

She felt no sense of satisfaction, as she had thought all along she might have done.

She felt no sense of achievement, or vindication, as she felt had driven her along over these months and days of planning, working, grief and grim determination.

In truth, she felt nothing.

She gazed out the cockpit window, up into the blue calm of the sky above.

Then looked down on the huddled, wretched sobbing man before her.

Her hand in her pocket pressed the button of the small electronic remote she had constructed over all those nights in the flat in the Royal Mile in Edinburgh.

And the electronic signal was sent to the explosive box

she had concealed in the fuselage of the Learjet.
There came an enormous noise.
Then utter blackness.

CHAPTER SIXTY TWO

After the media photographs, showing Granger with the Swilcan bridge and burn, so full of memories for him now, and the old Clubhouse and Hamilton Hall in the background, they put several microphones in his face.

"Give us your reactions, Jack!"

Granger looked up and away, back to the Old Course Hotel and the fairways he had just played.

"This is the finest round of golf I've ever played, and at the home of golf too. This week'll stay in my memory for ever I think. When I took 37 over the outward nine I thought I'd had it. I thought McAvon had it sewn up with his 35."

"Yes, but you seemed to be a new man after the ninth."

Granger smiled, looking at Laura and Amy.

"Yes, I was. I knew I'd have my work cut out, when McAvon had caught up and was shaping to go ahead of me even further today."

"And yet McAvon's outward round of 35 wasn't even good enough to hold you, was it?"

Granger smiled and shook his head.

"No. Nothing could stand in my way from the 10th on. My final nine holes of 29 was just fantastic. Pure bliss, Sheer heaven and satisfaction."

"This is your first major victory since May, isn't it? And did you ever think you'd add a third Open after the others?"

Granger bowed his head.

"Funnily, yes. Over the past few months my play tailed off dismally and I lost all confidence for a while, as you know. This happens to you after a real setback. Especially when you've got people staring, cameras watching your every move, helicopters above you, out even on a practice round. Life can be so hellish at times when you're down. But nobody pays attention to a loser, not for long.

I always had the idea at the back of my mind that my old self would come back. Stronger, more secure than before, and after the ninth here, as you saw, I managed to pick myself up and get on with it."

"Would your wife have anything to do with that?"

"Bet your bottom dollar! My darling wife Laura. And without doubt my lovely, determined daughter Amy, her fiancé Greg Walsh, my caddie George Orr and manager Mark Meekin, and all those who've wished me well and stood by me"

The commentator smiled.

"You more than picked yourself up and got on with it. You smashed the opposition!

CHAPTER SIXTY THREE

Out over mid-Atlantic the pilot of an eastbound 747, 6000 feet above the Learjet, had witnessed and reported the flash of an explosion below him and a blossoming red fireball as Diack's plane burst into a ball of flame. Debris and smoking parts fell, fluttering, sliding down towards the ocean, now in sunlight, now in gloom. All of them to disappear, as if they had never been, without trace into the bleak, grey expanse below.

CHAPTER SIXTY FOUR

The first shots on that little historic Swilcan Bridge, with the 18th, Hamilton and the R&A Clubhouse in the background, were of dad, arm in arm with Laura on one side and me, Amy on the other.

For the next shots Granger called in Mark Meekin and Greg, then insisted on one more final shot.

Of Greg and me.

So many others could have shared this final moment with us, dad and I were thinking.

There was one more person dad never knew about, but should have been there too.

Lisa Brand.